The Wooing of Ozma Book

Book One in the Umbrella Man in Oz Series

By

Charles Phipps

This book is a work of fiction. Places, events, and situations in this story are purely fictional. Any resemblance to actual persons, living or dead, is coincidental.

© 2002 by Charles Phipps. All rights reserved.

No part of this book may be reproduced, stored in a retrieval system, or transmitted by any means, electronic, mechanical, photocopying, recording, or otherwise, without written permission from the author.

ISBN: 1-4033-5726-9 (e-book)
ISBN: 1-4033-5727-7 (Paperback)
ISBN: 1-4033-5728-5 (Rocket Book)

Library of Congress Control Number: 2002093521

This book is printed on acid free paper.

Printed in the United States of America
Bloomington, IN

1stBooks — rev. 09/23/02

Prelude

Ozma, the Queen of Oz was the most beautiful, caring, intelligent, passionate, wondrous, loving, and curiously lonely woman in the Fairy Lands. As the shimmering goddess took a moment to stare out her window at the Emerald City that was her home, she mused on exactly why this was the case. It was a cool summer's night outside with the rainstorm that had ruined her parade earlier still pouring down buckets of water on the grand city's streets. Her palace chambers were completely silent and it was very conductive to a woman thinking about herself and loneliness.

'I have no lack of friends. The Hungry Tiger, Jack Pumpkinhead, the Cowardly Lion, dear dear Dorothy, the Sawhorse, the Scarecrow, my mentor Glinda, and so many other wonderful personages. Yet I find myself still feeling a great hole in my heart for someone else that does not exist in my life,' Ozma thought. Ozma gazed down on the many teeming citizens of the wonderful city, all dressed in green trying to get to their homes after the festivities to hold up til the end of the rain. Her eyes caught a glimpse of one particular couple in distress. They were lifting up their child who had accidentally broken his toy emerald kitten in getting out of the rain. They ran a shop which sold animate toys and the cat seemed was very irritated by being split in half.

'I am not a fool. I know what this hollowness is within my heart and I can give it a name here and now: I am lonely for love,' Ozma thought the word with some trace of embarrassment and more than a little mischievousness in her eyes. The citizens of Oz had long been divided on her marrying or falling in love. All it seemed, wanted her to marry no one, while each secretly either wanted to marry her or had a friend they thought it would be grand for her to marry. It would be wonderful if Ozma and her people had all agreed on this friend and personage for her to love but since they all had a different one in mind they came to the consensus it was better to keep the position open forever.

'And now I have vowed never to marry and love. It seems sometimes that it is the best course of action...and yet other times, it seems, such words ring as hollow and horrible as the vow at heart is,' Ozma mused. It had been an order of the kingdom that she should not take a consort because it prevented so many young Winkies, Munchkins, Quadlings, even Flying Monkeys and Nomes from comming to the Palace to court her. Yet it was a violation of the highest law in Oz for anyone to be unhappy.

"And I am unhappy," Ozma sighed. The ruler of Oz twirled around in her her room sadly before plopping herself onto her bed.

Ozma could remember one time when such thoughts of marriage were realistic, and she had hoped that she might find some kind of true love at last. However, the wisdom of the faeries precluded such, at thousands of years in age many fairies chose never to take brides or husbands and live lives for the sake of their dances or art or subjects. When Ozma had thought of being in love she had been a being both distant and close to Ozma's heart: her prior self, Tip. Tip had lived long enough as a boy to dream of escaping Mombi and marrying some Ozian lady but he had been a simple boy of low education, ambition, and good heart. Ozma faced many more difficulties as Queen. In a way she missed Tip and wished he could be here, though he'd make a poor husband for a princess, Ozma thought, he would have gotten along with Dorothy and perhaps would have found love there.

"Hahahaha." Ozma let her tinkling laughter ring like a bell as she realized how absurd her fancy had become. In lieu of imagining the perfect husband she had decided to play matchmaker with her best friend and a boy who had never actually existed. Rising to comb her hair this evening, Ozma pulled out her magical silver combs with their emerald teeth to begin the one thousand strokes her hair required. It was tedious work but a Queen had to look stately. Strangely people accepted that 'I have to comb my hair a thousand times' better as an excuse not to attend matters of state than 'I need time to think'. Ozma wondered if Dorothy, who was now nearly one hundred to Ozma's one thousand, but still was a young girl, had similar thoughts about marriage and resolved to ask her about it sometime.

"Perhaps I am too old," Ozma said looking into her mirror. No one in Oz aged unless they desired to do so after all. While some men seventy five looked the way men from Dorothy's world looked at that age (all stooped over and hobbled to look respectable), other more sane men chose to live thousands of years never a day over ten to twenty. Ozma herself chose to live for the most part at the age of fifteen, the final year before a person cast away all vestiges of childlike innocence to complete the transformation to adulthood.

However good a perspective this gave Ozma on life, her body still had entered womanhood and she often dreamed of completing the transformation. An Ozma of eighteen or twenty would certainly be the most lovely creature a man could ever known or desire, the reason Ozma never considered it for long. If the monarch of Oz had a true love she would certainly not mind growing older to be his wife in form and soul as only an adult could be, but she had no desire to break men's hearts as other faeries seemed to take pleasure in doing within less pleasant lands. The thought of growing younger had its own appeal to that she might cast away such adult thoughts but Ozma enjoyed them enough that it was as repellant as its reverse.

"Glinda, I wonder if you ever loved or married," Ozma thought as she continued her strokes and reached a hundred combs. The Good Witch of the South was certainly a woman and a very beautiful one at that. Yet, all men of Oz had learned that she had no interest in seeking one as a spouse. Whether it was because they were beneath her notice, or it was as Ozma suspected, and Glinda already had a sweetheart (or perhaps one she had lost long ago and still mourned) the result was the same and Glinda had no visible lover. It had been a sensible precaution for Glinda to have only girls in her palace, truly, because in either case she would certainly have any male servants fall instantly in love with her. While the thought was amusing, it would also be very troublesome. If Glinda wanted her bath water drawn or slippers fetched, it would be difficult to get such things done with the men fighting amongst themselves, or ignoring their duties to write poems, pick flowers (which was Ozma thought was just horrid), and other things Ozma had learned were part of the silliness men engaged in to show they cared, rather than simply say it. It was better that Glinda did not have such trouble as Ozma would have to deal with should she ever become an adult.

"I suppose, Lady Glinda, if you ever needed a lover he would have to be the most powerful magician in the world as well…or a complete humbug," Ozma smiled weakly as she reached two hundred brushes. Her reflection was very silent tonight as she was doing her own hair but Ozma trusted her with all of her secrets and she occasionally confided some of her own to Ozma. The magical mirror had been a gift from Queen Zixi and brought to life the reflection of whoever gazed in it. Ozma oftened wondered what went on beyond the looking glass but she was resolved to read Lewis Caroll before she explored at any length the other side. She'd gone on too many adventures without proper fore-research.

It was another problem of Ozma's that though she might love a man, if she married any man he would have to be her equal or the lowest of the low. The former would be troubling indeed as Ozma was quite certain that such a man who was possessed of her age, beauty, wisdom, great magic, strength in spirit, and nobility should not be shackled to merely being the consort of a woman who ruled her kingdom eternally. Such a man would grow quickly bored with play and paradise to seek out great adventures and kingdoms of his own. That would make Ozma very lonely, as they would be apart most of the time. It was not a difficult thing to imagine that she might share ruler-ship with her husband but Ozma knew her people best, and she had no desire to abandon half of her own day to someone else.

"What about the complete humbug?" Ozma's reflection asked as Ozma reached three hundred and thirty three strokes.

The idea had seemed at first ridiculous to Ozma, that she might marry the lowest of the low but the ruler of Oz was not ashamed that she was a magnet to misfits. Those who were ruled by their flaws, be they a conscience when fat babies beckon, courage only when it is needed, or a head which is in constant need of replacing due to spoilage, were always near Ozma's heart because it was from these troubles they became great. Even her friends who were not misfits had qualities about them that set them apart from the other people in Oz who gazed upon her so adoringly. Glinda was close to Ozma because she was the greatest in the land, while Dorothy was her best friend because she was so perfectly ordinary. A person who saw the Queen of the magical land as a person first, then her title, was a rare commodity and one both frightening and wonderful.

"Yes I could marry someone like that…if they could juggle," Ozma smirked as she reached eight hundred and fifty-three. It was a mean thing to smirk in Oz, it sometimes seemed, because a smirk was a secret smile of triumph instead of a public one. Ozma, after stopping, so, wondered if her smirk hadn't caused some terrible calamity in Oz. Everything she did seemed to so perfectly reflect something wonderful usually, but that was when she did something good. The Queen dearly hoped the reverse was not true but having rarely, if ever, done something wrong it was difficult to tell. In any case she didn't mean that juggling of objects would be a requirement of her love, though it would certainly be nice if he could, she meant that he could juggle respect for her and adulation.

"I had best check the Magic Picture to see if something in Oz has been effected by my smirk," Ozma resolved as she put her comb down at nine hundred ninety nine. The Monarch's reflection finished her own combing then reached through the window and stroked Ozma's hair from behind while the ruler of Oz got up. Rain rarely helped anyone's feelings regarding immenate calamity "Thank you," Ozma looked back at her reflection.

The mirror Ozma then nodded sagely and said, "You're welcome."

Ozma checked the land of Oz for inhabitants who were troubled and saw that a poor fox had been beaten quite painfully by some of Bellina's chickens, a Munchkin's dinner had burned, and the emerald cat who had been broken was having difficulty finding glue along with a competent craftsmen to put him back together. Ozma had no idea which of these events, if any, had been caused by her smirking, but resolved to make up for it by inviting all of them to the palace for the royal treatment tomorrow to make up for it. Ozma ignored the troubles being caused by the rain thus far since she suspected quite rightly that the storm had no natural cause and little to do with her sly smile. It was then a thought hit her, and she turned to the Magic Picture as she said a single sentence: "Show me my soul-mate and true love," Ozma blinked, waiting for the response. She smiled whimsically as the magic picture showed the doorways to her room with the words OZ imprinted upon them in beautiful shining gold letters. Fate had revealed itself that she would always be in love with her kingdom, and that was what her destiny would be from this day forward. Ozma proceeded to her doorway and pulled it open before shutting her eyes and heading out. It was a melancholy moment and one that required the utmost dignity.

"Farewell my dream…OOoooph!" Ozma said as she suddenly tripped head over heads and landed on her posterior. Looking backwards, after checking to see if she was still regal (she was), Ozma tried to see at what had tripped her and found her self gazing upon a young man who was leaning over just nearly out of sight of the Magic Picture.

"Oh pardon me madam…errr…are you Princess Ozma? I was leaning over to pick up an emerald which had fallen off your door. I was told to speak with you about…some things," the man said in a bit of a shy voice. Ozma grinned, which was entirely different than a smirk, but had the same connotations without the possible disaster.

"Yes, I am indeed sir." Ozma rose to her destiny.

Chapter One

Earlier that Day...

In the kingdom of Zo there was much unhappiness. The kingdom was not like most kingdoms because it was a fairy kingdom. Unlike its cousin in the land of Oz however, Zo did not benefit from its magic, but instead suffered greatly for it. Its ruler was a vain, tempermental, and otherwise unpleasant young woman whose moods made everything the kingdom floated over dark and stormy. The kingdom of Zo, you see, floated above the clouds both you and I take for granted in the sky and its ruler disliked everything below her tiny palace. The main reason was because Zo was not much bigger than a city and the world below was vast.

"IGOR!" the Princess's shrill voice rang throughout the Obsidian City.

"YES, PRINCESS ZOAM!" Igor Lackey, whose name had guaranteed his position in life, came up to the gigantic throne of Princess Zoam. Zoam was monarch of Zo and its absolute commander and chief in all things nasty, which was everything.

Igor was not like other residents in Zo because he was not a hideous man, nor slouched over, and in fact quite handsome. Despite the encouragements of the fellows of his court who valued ugliness, Igor preferred to be comely in front of his Princess. The only things that kept Igor from being kicked out by outraged Zo nobles were that he often had a conniving look on his face and wore a very threatening military uniform covered in medals for presumably unpleasant things. Having inherited it from his father Evile Lackey, the uniform was quite well covered.

"My kingdom is too small, Igor, and I want you to fix it," Princess Zoam said pouting. Princess Zoam, like Igor was not unpleasant to look at. Indeed Zoam was almost breathtakingly beautiful, which had very little to do with being a good person (she was not) but quite a lot to do with her being one of the Fairy Folk of whom all are very beautiful indeed. Dressed in a plain black gown with two lilies in her hair, which the only flowers to grow in Zo, Princess Zoam had long black tresses and a gold crown with a circle and a Z emblazoned upon it. The Princess was sitting on her obsidian throne and tapping her magic bronze wand against her throne quite testily. For those who knew of the Princess Ozma, who was unknown in the Land of Zo, she was furthermore the spitting image of the great and glorious leader of Fairyland's most wonderous kingdom.

Igor sighed at her majesty's request. "Your Highness, the Harpies, Slavercruds, and Hissing-Wings are tired from your last attempt to expand your kingdom. The other clouds we attack simply do not last long enough to be of any real value and we always lose sight of them whenever a strong wind blows past. Now, let me brew you another thunderstorm." Igor was quite talented at all things mechanical and had found the terrible winds, rain, and lighting he brewed up for Zoam were among the few things which made her happy. If you ever have a particularly bad rainstorm that the weatherman didn't predict, you may want to keep watch for the black towers of Zo.

The Wooing of Ozma

"NO!" Princess Zoam pointed her wand at her court jester E. Bused and transformed him into a gigantic toad for little purpose other than the fact she wanted to turn him into a giant toad. "Am I not the rightful queen of Zo? Does not the great crown of my ancestor King Zo rest upon my head? I demand that you find me a kingdom to conquer to add to Zo and I demand you do it now!"

Igor put his hand to his head and sighed deeply as E. Bused hopped off toward the dungeons. "Very well your majesty, give me a moment…" Igor didn't know of any countries that could keep his lady's interest in the sky that they could conquer, the rulers of the Fairy Sky Kingdoms were powerful and unforgiving folk. The land of mortals only kept the Princess's interests for brief times and while on occasion the princess fell in love with mortal men like the one presently in the dungeons she rarely enjoyed looking at them for long. It was one of the reasons Zo was always on the move. The Princess could not stand to look at the same country for more than a few days. Igor only knew of a few fairy kingdoms on the ground as well. "Wait, Your Highness, I may have it!"

Princess Zoam was already munching on a granola bar and apparently had forgotten about the entire conversation. The young man she had captured had introduced her to it and Igor had been stuck discovering ways to find the admittedly delicious food for the Princess. "Hmmm?" She asked.

"Expanding your kingdom may lie in the very history of our land. Do you remember so many centuries past when Zo was but merely the clouds above another land?" Igor raised a hand into the air.

Charles Phipps

"No. I wasn't born yet," Princess Zoam said, looking annoyed.

"I mean…ugh. Very well, long ago, Princess, before our tiny city and its' castle were built, the clouds were merely hovering clouds over the greater land of Oz. The kingdom of Oz was ruled by a line of Kings named Oz and a line of Queens and Princesses named Ozma. Eventually, however, one of the Queens gave birth to a pair of twins who could not both be named Oz…"

Igor stopped as Zoam interrupted.

"Why not if the King was already named Oz?" Princess Zoam asked blinking.

Igor stopped to ponder that one. "I'm afraid I don't know, Your Highness. In any case, the present King Oz hit upon the idea to name the younger of the Princes Zo instead of Oz. The older brother, Prince Oz, grew up to be honest, forthright, courteous, and fair while the younger brother, Prince Zo, grew up to be arrogant, cruel, greedy, and mean."

"All great virtues," The Princess nodded.

"Indeed, Your Royalness, but for some reason King Oz did not want to give the entirety of the kingdom to Prince Zo. Instead he offered the Prince the sky above the land and allowed him to pick what citizens he'd like to accompany him to build his kingdom. The Prince chose those whom appealed to his nature and he ended up with nearly all the ill humored, backstabbing, and otherwise unpleasant individuals in the land," Igor nodded at the Princess.

"What a lovely story," Princess Zoam smiled. "I don't see how that increases my kingdom,

The Wooing of Ozma

HOWEVER!" She shouted the last word and the force of her breath sent Igor down to the floor.

"Don't you see Your Greatness? The beauty of the faeries has always guaranteed that the Kings of Oz and Daughters Ozma resemble one another and surely, with your magic, you'd be able to pass yourself off as the current Princess of the Land. You'd be able to take over, thus ruling both Zo and Oz together!" Igor smiled at the cleverness of his plan.

"Yes, but Igor, what if it's currently a King Oz ruling Oz?" Princess Zoam questioned.

Igor blanched. He was hoping that she wouldn't ask that. "We'll deal with that when we get there, Your Magnificence." Princess Zoam smiled at the thought of ruling over a land that actually would last longer than the next big wind and giggled just the slightest bit. "Igor, brew up a very big storm for this event! In the meantime, I'm going to go visit my pet mortal in the dungeons." The Princess rose to do that very thing.

Igor sighed, more than a little jealous that Zoam never took the time to abuse him the same way as she did her mortals.

***

Milo Starling sat in the back of his cage and hummed a rather catchy tune lightly to himself, which helped pass the time and distract him from the fact he was in a cage. Milo was possessed of a pleasant personality but plain mind. This that was not to say he was stupid but that he was extremely frank, honest, and forthright. An insurance salesman's son from Kentucky he had never been in trouble before, at least to the extent of being kidnapped by an evil princess of a flying country. Truth be told, he imagined even if he hadn't been a pleasant plain son of a insurance salesman there was little chance the young man would have been prepared for something like this.

Milo was not a man that you might generally notice in a crowd but there was a nobility in his features that shined through if you bothered to look at him closely. Tall, straight, thin with strawberry blonde hair and green eyes, there was a bit of fairy to his features that might have been traced back to the land of Scotland his family hailed from. He was dressed in his Sunday clothes and was currently paging through the copy of the Good Book he had in his hands when Zo's forces had kidnapped him. At his side was his umbrella which sadly had served as little defense against the forces of the sinister rainmakers.

"Psssst!" a rather loud voice rang through the dungeon, which contained nothing but obsidian walls and empty cages save his own.

Milo was about to start flipping through his copy of the Good Book and wondered what could be the source of this latest disturbance. The Kentuckian then looked over to see the curious sight of a gigantic toad in the costume of a court jester standing right in front of his prison cell.

"Ummm Hello," Milo said, trying to avoid staring. Since he had come to be a prisoner in the land of Zo he'd had quite a lot of his views challenged, however nothing that had made him question the virtues of being polite.

"I've come to rescue you. Hey, what are you reading?" The toad hopped over and grabbed the keys off the wall.

The Wooing of Ozma

"The Good Book," Milo replied simply.

"It must be extremely interesting if that's its title," The Toad said as he unlocked Milo's cage.

"In part, Goodsir. It is, however, full of advice which I'm memorizing. For instance, 'Happiness comes to those who are fair to others and always just and good.' Is an excellent quote," Milo pointed out a passage in the book.

"What if your happiness comes from being unfair to others and being unjust and bad?" the toad asked curiously.

"I'll have to look up another passage to see about that," Milo crawled out of his cage and dusted himself off. He then proceeded to remove his copy of the Good Book and his umbrella, which he had been opening before his unfortunate transportation up to Zo and still hadn't been folded properly.

"Righto." the toad man gave a webbed thumb up.

"Thank you very much for saving me. However may I ask why you are helping me?" Milo didn't wish to seem ungrateful but he did wonder about the people of Zo after having encountered no one but the nastiest of it's people since his arrival in Fairyland. Besides finding out his motivations might be the start of a wonderful friendship.

"I'm the Court Jester E. Bused, which would explain the clothes…" The Toadman stopped in mid sentence to point at his costume "but Her Nastiness has been transforming me for years and this is the last straw for me. I think it is probably a good idea to release her other prisoners as well but I don't know of any but for the entire population and freeing them would be problematic I think," E. Bused said as he jingled the bells on his costume just the slightest bit and grabbed a nearby fly with his tongue.

"Uck. I can see your problem," Milo nodded.

E. Bused went on, "I mean really I rather enjoyed being turned into a dragon and the giant rat was at least scary. Really being a big fluffy kitten is very enjoyable too because people pet you a lot. Heck, when you're black you can even cross their path to give them bad luck, but really what's the fun in being a giant...." E. Bused stopped in mid sentence to flick another fly out of the air with his tongue.

Milo blanched as he looked over his clothes and grabbed the umbrella he had in his cell with him. The objects were entirely inappropriate for escape. Milo had been going to church at the time he was kidnapped by Princess Zo's flying monsters and had not prepared for escaping a flying island. "Listen, Mr. Bused, I don't mean to be a bother. But, while your transformation history is actually quite fascinating, I am rather concerned we should be concentrating on escaping this Dungeon now. I'm sure it won't be long until Princess Zoam or one of her minions arrives for my daily abuse."

The sound of thunder and lightning that suddenly filled the halls of the palace did not entirely drown out the sound of Princess Zoam's descent down the stairs. Mostly because it was accompanied by her crying out "Yooo Hooo! Milo! I've come to talk about our upcoming wedding!" Milo, having little desire to marry an evil Princess, no matter how beautiful, immediately grabbed E. Bused by the arm and began to run quickly down the hall of the dungeon and up the steps on the opposite side.

The Wooing of Ozma

"I didn't know that you were going to marry the Princess!" E. Bused said as they ran past the guards of the Obsidian Palace, who preferred to ignore any people running through the halls than rather give chase. The benefits for being guards in an evil fairy's castle aren't very good you know.

"Neither did I!" Milo sighed, continuing into the streets of Zo. The entire city was made of obsidian, but it wasn't polished and frequently cracked. The people dressed in rags and dirt with weapons, eye patches, and fake black teeth being the current fashion.

"STOP THEM! BY ORDER OF THE PRINCESS ZO!" Princess Zoam shouted behind them and lifted up her bronze wand, firing bolts of transformation force madly with unintended effects. A old man whacking a child for trying to steal his wooden leg was turned into a majestic eagle and flew away happy for the first time in his life. A crotchety baker was transformed into a powerful lion which immediately started chasing away his rude customers with glee. The third, a lonely young man, was immediately turned into a pretty young girl who would never want for attention. Thus the escape of the two fugitives of Zo was aided by many of the inhabitants of Zo throwing their bodies in front of the Princess's magic wand in hopes of being transformed into something less miserable.

"Ha! We're almost free! Down with Princess Zoam! Up with Good guys! PPpppppphhhttt!" E. Bused took the time to stick out his exceptionally long tongue at the Princess and give her perhaps the greatest raspberry ever.

"Unfortunately I would not necessarily count on the free part," Milo said as their trek came to an end a

Charles Phipps

few minutes later. The Kingdom of Zo was not large but unfortunately it came to a very long drop at the end, instead of exiting to a more hospitable land. If it had led to a better land the population would have long since left.

"Ribbit!" E. Bused said a rather very rude word in Toad, who of course have very little to do with Frogs because people are always mistaking one for the other but that is neither here nor there.

The sky above and below the pair of escapees was already full of storms, and soon filled with harpies, slavercruds, and hissing-wings. Monsters of course are considerably less lazy than the guards in the pursuit of doing unpleasant things to people who have offended the Princess.

"Oh dear," Milo said, looking around as E. Bused wrapped his wet and slimy hands around his new (and only) friend. "I'm afraid, Mister Bused, I can think of only one thing to do right now."

E. Bused looked up. "What's that sir?"

"Scream," Milo said as E. Bused nodded, and they cried out together in a chorus of "HELP!"

***

Polychrome joyously danced on her father the rainbow as she tried to avoid focusing on the rather nasty sight of Zo not that far away. Her father could appear as a mortal, a handsome fairy king, or as a leprechaun, but avoided those forms for the pure beauty of colors when he could. Polychrome on the other hand enjoyed wearing the shape of a pretty blonde girl with a scintillating colored dress. It was the Rainbow Fairies job to bring joy to people and they

The Wooing of Ozma

spent a lot of their time following the wicked storm makers in Zo across the Earth and Fairyland. It was then that the Rainbow could brighten up the days of those whom the Rainmakers terrified with their storm machines.

"La da deee…" Polychrome sang, smiling as she stopped when she heard a rather curious cry for help. It was rather unusual to hear anything up in the sky but for the birds chirping and the awful sound of thunder that Zo made. To Polychrome's her knowledge no birds or clouds in this region spoke Ozish either which of course is plain English.

"Father let's go see what's going on," Polychrome said, and the rainbow quickly passed by the ugly monsters that Zo made use of and she came face to face with two rather bizarre looking creatures for birds or clouds. In fact they resembled a drenched human being in his Sunday clothes or a giant toad in a jester's outfit.

"Hello," The first one said executing a rather sweeping formal bow. He was a young man, unless he was from someplace where nobody ever aged, and was just entering adulthood. He was actually rather pretty to Polychrome's eye and she had seen alot of mortals in her many long years of life. It only took a moment to determine he was in fact a man and not a bird or cloud, but the figure didn't look like any of the horrible inhabitants of Zo that Polychrome had seen. They were a nasty folk constantly pelting her friends the birds and clouds in their attempts to conquer everything in the sky. The young man also had an umbrella, which was forbidden as far as the Rainbow Fairy knew in Zo.

Charles Phipps

"Salutations," Polychrome said. "Did you hear someone cry for help?"

"That would be us ma'am," A giant Toad said. He was covered in bells and the outlandish attire of a court jester, as if being a toad wasn't funny enough.

"Oh, are you in trouble?" Polychrome asked, knowing what that was like.

Milo coughed into his hand and looked toward the terrible monsters, which were flying around the rainbow. Monsters as a rule didn't like the Rainbow and Polychrome always had wondered why. After all, her father was always warm and pleasant plus she and her sisters were always kind.

"Miss, it's a rather long story…" Milo said.

Polychrome crossed her arms to wait and hear it "But if it is within your power, could you please take us someplace a bit more hospitable like the Good Samaritan? We're in a difficult situation with the Princess and since we didn't do anything wrong, we'd rather like to avoid her wrath," Milo explained as best he could in the limited amount of time they had.

Polychrome had often in her life found herself in difficult situations like accidentally wandering off the rainbow but each time someone had been nice enough to help her. The Rainbow Fairy decided that this time she would return the favor to these nice mortals. Her father the Rainbow seemed to want to help them as well.

So, offering her hand to both of them, she took them onboard and they set sail down the colorful lights down to the Earth below. A trip that would take them well away from the powers of Princess Zo.

The Wooing of Ozma

"What's a Samaritan?" Polychrome asked out of genuine curiosity

Chapter Two

Milo landed with a thud on the ground in the Country of the Munchkins. E. Bused landed a few seconds later and Polychrome gently glided to the ground with little effort after them. The group had the unfortunate luck to land in the Forrest of Nasty Ornery Oaks. Thankfully, they had caught them in one of their rare quiet moods so it was actually not so unfortunate after all.

"Bye Daddy! I'll see you in a few days." Polychrome waved to the retreating form of her father in the sky. Polychrome had visited the land of Oz numerous times in the past and her father the Rainbow King was not going to worry about leaving her there for a few days to visit her friends there. It also was such a nice country that Polychrome was sure that her new friends would be happy to stay there forever after.

Meanwhile Milo slowly got up and tried desperately to straighten himself out. His hair was completely straight in the air, his balance was off, and his hands were shaking from Polychrome's magical trip. "My, you're probably the first human who's ever ridden a rainbow before." Polychrome smiled.

"I'm certain therefore, that I must be the first giant toad to have ever ridden a rainbow. I wouldn't recommend it!" E. Bused said, laying on the ground and not bothering to get up as he spoke.

Polychrome looked hurt "Let us not complain about the trip the lovely lady has given us, E. Bused. Our position here is infinitely better than our position…there…wherever…here and there is." Milo

The Wooing of Ozma

made a vague gesture with his hands and tried to straighten his umbrella, which had completely folded up.

"You're in the Land of Oz now. It is the home of my friends who live on the ground like you. I'm sure the Ruler of Oz Princess Ozma and her friend Princess Dorothy would be happy to help you out. They've helped many people against icky folk like those in Zo before." Polychrome grin grew even wider.

Milo nodded his head. "Er, thank you very much." Truth be told, Milo had very little desire to deal with any more royalty after his initial encounters with them. Had not the Good Book admonished kings as thieves and takers of children in it?

"Do you think she might be able to turn me back into…well no, I'd rather not be turned back into a man anymore," E. Bused said as he plopped himself up on his webbed feet again.

"What's wrong with being a man? I'm rather fond of it myself." Milo picked his glasses from his pocket and discovered, to his dismay, that one of his lenses had been broken by the fall. Still he decided that viewing this land clearly with one good eye was much better than viewing it foggily with both.

"Well, maybe that's because you are tall and straight. My ancestors are Munchkins, however, and according to our legends they were a diabolical and cruel race with huge pointy teeth and long claws to compensate for their short size. The Old legends say we were exiled because we had none of these qualities." E. Bused made an ugly face as his tongue swished about in the air.

"How horrid," Milo said to Polychrome's giggles.

"This is the country of the Munchkins and they're very nice people one and all," Polychrome said.

"Well, if they're nice people one and all I'm sure we can forgive the pointy teeth and long claws." Milo tossed his straightened out umbrella over his left shoulder. "I don't suppose we have much of a choice if we are to ever find our way out of this predicament."

"Predica-what?" E. Bused asked.

"Never mind. Lead the way to Queen Ozma, her King, and Princess Dorothy, Lady...errrr." Milo gestured with his umbrella as Polychrome smiled and began walking towards the Yellow Brick Road. Unfortunately, she had no idea how to reach from this point in Munchkin country, but she was content just to be walking. In truth, her walking more resembled dancing, which she never stopped doing, even for a moment.

"Actually, Ozma doesn't have a King unless you count her father, Mister...." Polychrome stopped as she realized that in their haste they had neglected to introduce themselves. That was in fact why Milo was shaking his umbrella at her, hoping she might tell him her name.

"Milo, Milo T. Starling at your service milady." Milo gave another sweeping bow to her. He'd been taught from the beginning of his life by his mother that if you couldn't be dramatic you might as well not be anything.

"I am Polychrome, the Daughter of the Rainbow," Polychrome introduced herself with a duplicate of his bow, which was quite silly in her mind. "And thank you very much. If I need anything done, I'll be glad to have you do it."

The Wooing of Ozma

Milo stopped to think about that for a second, before he shrugged, wondering what he had just agreed to. Whatever he had promised in his greeting was probably the least he could do for Polychrome's good deed however.

"E. Bused. The E stands for Easily and my middle name is Athletically. I am a master juggler, jumper, tumbler, acrobat, stage magician, knife tosser, joke teller, sword swallower, fire breather, and I can even sing." The giant toad man began to perform an aria in Italian, which immediately caused Milo to cover E. Bused's mouth with both hands to Polychrome's considerable relief.

"Please don't do that again." Milo shuddered as they began to walk down the forested paths.

"I didn't say I was a master singer." The Toadman did a series of jumps and tumbles around the group. "It's a pity the Princess Zoam is only entertained by turning me into things," E. Bused sighed and continued to move with the group.

"I'm sure you'll be a big hit with Ozma...as long as you don't sing. She is the supreme ruler of Oz and everyone loves her dearly." Polychrome began to tell the pair about the many fantastic characters of Oz, who I am sure that those who will be reading this are quite well knowledgeable about. Since listing all of them would take a substantial portion of this book, I shall simply say that they talked for hours.

Milo and E. Bused learned much that day and were greatly impressed with the wonders that the Fairy Country had to offer.

***

Charles Phipps

Meanwhile, Princess Ozma leaned on the railing of her palace's balcony and watched the parade, which Jellia Jamb as her chamberlain (as well as housekeeper) had arranged for "No particular reason." The Parade had quickly transformed into a celebration of "Ozma day." Green and gold banners emblazoned with the royal seal followed by yellow, red, blue, and purple ones. Visitations for Ozma day included the King of the Flying Monkeys, the Three Adepts who ruled over the Flatheads, and the Royal family of Ix. It was very nice of them to travel all this way but it was quite boring in their kingdoms anyway and Jellia had promised free food. More truthfully, they were here to honor a queen who had done the Continent of Imagination greater service than any other.

"Isn't an absolutely wonderful Ozma Week?" Jellia smiled as she stood next to her royal highness. The Chief Most Maid of the Emerald City was currently dressed in a pretty emerald gown with two blue opal studded J's on the bottom of her dress.

"Ozma Week?" Ozma asked, looking at Jellia.

"Well everyone is having such an absolutely wonderful time enjoying the 'No particular reason' parade that I decided to make it for you, and since everyone absolutely loves you so very much and so many people are still arriving, we decided to make it a celebration to last all week." Jellia stared and waved across the field to where the machine man Tik Tok was marching with Omby Amby.

Since Omby Amby had been retired as the entire collective sum of the Oz army he had taken upon the duties of Emerald City Police Force, Fire Department,

The Wooing of Ozma

and Royal Guard. This meant roughly that he had as little to do as before.

"Well, I suppose that's nice, since everyone is enjoying themselves," Ozma said as she looked down on the parade and felt a rather vague disquiet that showed on her face. Truth be told, Ozma had felt this disquiet steadily growing for some time now until it was practically impossible to ignore.

"Yes, and when Ozma Week is done, I think we can make it Ozma Month and then Ozma Year. In fact, everyone is having such a great time, the Scarecrow and I have thought about arranging it so every day is Ozma Day!" Jellia Jamb giggled.

"Certainly not!" Ozma glanced up in shock.

Jellia blinked at the Queen very surprised "But Your Majesty, everyone is enjoying themselves so much getting dressed in their best clothes, or having new clothes made. With the music, merriment, dancing, and feasting, everyone I'm sure would love to celebrate your reign forever."

"I think they would enjoy the music, merriment, dancing, and feasting even if it was for the Nome King, Jellia," Ozma said with a slight smile.

"True enough, though they would at least make the showing of not liking it as a favor to you. You've brought the kingdom so much happiness that I'm sure it's the least anyone could do. In fact, I'd even avoid dessert at a banquet for the Nome King." Jellia nodded her head and crossed her arms in a show of defiance.

Ozma smiled at that. "Presuming that the dessert was something edible at his banquet and not poison or molten silver then I would not ask you to make such a sacrifice. No, as much as my people love me I would rather them not celebrate my life day in and day out. Surely it would grow monotonous if I everyone spent their days admiring me rather than something useful."

Jellia stopped for a moment to think about that. "Many couples in Oz consider it a unspoken duty of their position to admire, and consider it quite useful. In fact, as I understand it, those who do not admire their partners find their spouses extremely cross." She glanced over the parade as Glinda passed by and waved on her golden chariot drawn by swans.

Ozma blushed. "I would not condemn someone to be my spouse, I can assure you. Such a position I'm sure would be quite unpleasant with matters of state demanding that I never be completely free for them. I have no need of a king, and I'm sure he would not enjoy simply sitting around. Plus would not my friends feel slighted or jealous that I have someone else to devote my time to?" Ozma blinked as she saw Jellia staring at her. "Is something the matter Jellia?"

"My dear Princess Ozma, you are making excuses!" Jellia crossed her arms. "Couples always have such problems, and some would say that the first two are not problems at all, but ways of ensuring you do not go crazy at the sight of one another." Ozma blinked in surprise at that previously unknown side effect of marriage. "And for shame, thinking we wouldn't be happy for both of you! Surely someone you love and loves you back will be a firm friend to us as well," Jellia scolded her regent.

Ozma realized that the disquiet inside her was in small part due to loneliness and she wondered indeed why this was so when she had so many friends. Was having a companion, whom you loved as a husband,

The Wooing of Ozma

truly so much more important than friends or family? "Let us simply enjoy the parade, Jellia, and not discuss such things now."

It was then that the parade ceased, thanks to a crack of thunder and a sudden downpour of heavy rain that covered the Emerald City. The banners were soaked to wet towels. Terrible winds blew away hats and bonnets. The beautiful cakes prepared in honor of Ozma were turned into sludge. Ozma and Jellia immediately lifted themselves up and returned inside the palace as Ozma ordered Amby and the Cowardly Lion help the Tin man inside. The man of metal had rusted solid just outside the gates and for the Emperor of the Winkies that was quite embarrassing. After that was done, the Tin man was suitably oiled, and back to normal. Once everyone warmed themselves by Ozma's fireplace it was back to the celebration.

"This is not natural rain," The Wizard of Oz said, walking into Ozma's throne room where the ruler was sitting down and taking a break from the new feasting. The Wizard looked quite annoyed that his brand new waistcoat and tails were completely drenched and his remaining hair, prepared for this evening in a curled up fashion, drooped most comically.

"Why Wizard, whatever do you mean?" Ozma asked most curiously. Ozma did feel there was something strange about the rain, but had paid it no real attention until this moment.

"Your Majesty, permit me to speak on such things that I, as a man of many talents and magics, have observed weather patterns for a great many years as a professional balloonist." The Wizard wrung out some of the water from his coat onto Ozma's floor. "I can

Charles Phipps

assure you this morning I tested with my instruments the condition of the clouds, moisture, humidity, temperature, electricity, and ambient likelihood of a downpour and I confirmed to Jellia that it was most definitely not going to rain today."

"Yet it is," Ozma said, gesturing with her wand to her balcony as more water poured down and another disturbing crack of thunder echoed. Storms in Oz, to Ozma's knowledge, were never violent. This one tough was extremely angry sounding as if the clouds were fighting, which really was how lightning and thunder usually came about, but she'd put a stop to that among them sometime ago.

"Which leads me to believe that this storm is the product of someone using magic to tamper with the weather. At considerable cost to my getting further wet, I have done more tests with my instruments and discovered that the entire land of Oz is currently being rained upon at once. Something that in our entire history has never occurred before." The Wizard bowed his head.

"Which does not mean that it couldn't ever happen," Ozma pointed out. "Still, I tend to agree that this is the product of magic and not merely a very large drizzle. Since I can think of no one who would want to spoil my parade with a shower among those authorized to practice magic, I must think this is the work of someone most distinctly unauthorized and request that you investigate further. I shall ask the Lady Glinda to check her Book of Records for who in Oz may be causing this as well." Ozma put her hand to her head and frowned wondering who might be the responsible party. Many powerful and wicked Necromancers from

The Wooing of Ozma

the monstrous Lackey family to vile Scoodler shamans had been driven out of Oz over the years. Any one of them might be willing to break the ban on magic to return and seek revenge.

The Wizard nodded and Ozma thought of Dorothy, who was in Munchkin Country checking on the first sighting of a Snark Snark in years.

***

Meanwhile back in Zo, Princess Zoam was having what was probably best termed a fit. The northwest tower was where she most enjoyed having these fits because it was here that all of Igor's foul weather making machinery was located. The machines made the tower both drafty and cold which made a nice contrast to the heat of her anger. The sound of her screams also blended nicely with the clanging, banging, and puffing of the noxious gears, balloons, and vats of the machines. Igor was to the side of the room furiously pedaling the bicycle that operated the gears to create rain as he ran a wooden rattle down a long sheet of metal that helped in the creation of thunder. Hot acidic smoke from his weather maker blew from a whistle into his face, and if he had not been wearing his goggles he might have been blinded. As such, the henchman was merely irritated.

"Fools! Blunderers! Is there anyone more stupid in all of Zo than my subjects and guards?" Princess Zoam looked around for E. Bused. The Princess wanted to turn him into a fluffy white rabbit or a giant three headed hydra, or both so the latter could eat the former before she smacked her head and realized that his escape along with her new toy was the reason of her anger. Besides she wouldn't like the answer that was there was someone stupidier in Zo than her subjects in this very tower (Hint: It wasn't Igor).

"Your Most Powerfulness will forgive me if I remind you that I thought it was a very poor idea to bring a mortal here anyway. Besides, you will soon have enough people to transform from the prisoners we take in the Land of Oz. All we have to do is replace you as their queen and flood it so well that they are too muddled to resist," Igor said as he huffed and puffed from the strenuous exercise creating a monsoon entailed.

"Igor will forgive the Princess if she does not forgive him! I will have the people of Oz as my servants and toys, yes. I will probably change many of them into strange shapes, make them do bizarre tasks for my amusement, and stand in long lines and fill out embarrassing forms for no discernible purpose, but I would do that anyway! I want what I would have done to E. Bused and that lovely Milo had they not escaped as well!" Zoam cried and stamped her foot. The strength of the princess sent more rumbles down through Zo than all of Igor's machines could in a week. "Captain of the Guard! COME TO ME!"

Flapping in through the tower windows, the Captain of the Guard in Zo was a rather large hissing-wing. If I forgot to describe the Hissing-Wings earlier it is because they are not very pleasant to look upon (as their name might imply to you) and it's only with great difficulty that I tell you about them now. The Captain of the Guard was huge even by hissing-wing standards, and that is larger than a toucan and an ox put together. He had a large beak, terrible claws, and his most

The Wooing of Ozma

prominent feature was his wings, which had large holes in them that make the sound of hissing that gave their race its' name. These holes are not natural, but due the fact that they poke holes by crashing into sharp branches, rocks, and other objects on the ground. Hissing Wings, while very ferocious, love to crash. "Yessssssss Your Extreme Potentnessness, Prettyness, and Cruelness?" the beast-man said with a lisp.

"I want you to go throughout the land and seek out my lost toy and my court jester. The former you will recognize because he is the most handsome, wonderful, kind, and warm person in the world, and the next because he is a giant toad in a jester's costume."

The Princess tapped her bronze wand in her hand. The Hissing-Wing frowned and hissed in anger at her description. Hissing-Wings, despite their name, are not actually by nature bad, but actually quite pleasant. However the Captain of the Guard and his men had been brought up to terrorize the populous of Zo by Zoam's father and thus had never known anything but to be mean and enjoy it. Things like handsome, wonderful, kind, and warm were thus things that made this group of hissing-wings quite angry even though they'd never seen them personally.

"He is also carrying an umbrella," Igor said with distaste as he peddled faster and honked a nearby horn, causing lightning. The description of Milo Starling had infuriated him as well though for different reasons than the Captain of the Guard. Igor had a much different relationship with the Princess and it was prone to jealousy.

Charles Phipps

The flapping of the Captain's wings made a hissing sound as he backed away from Igor at the mention of the dreaded weapon. "Is there anything else your Most Beautiful Wickedness wishes?"

The Princess thought about this for a moment and then commanded him, "Fetch for me one of every creature in the Land of Oz. I will know in vivid detail just what sort of wonders and foes I will face once I am ruler of this land. Leave no stone unturned…"

"That will take many years milady," The Captain said.

"Very well, simply bring me one of every creature you can find," the Princess said, realizing it was quite silly. A rattle of the machine blasted behind her and she clapped her hands together in maniacal glee. Her kingdom was about to become one Oz sized realm larger.

The Wooing of Ozma
Chapter Three

Dorothy Gale looked at the Mayor of Munchkin Town, Thaddeus Bumhug. Thaddeus had a long-standing rivalry with the Mayor of Munchkinville that may have had something to do with the fact that the Mayor of Munchkinville was his brother. Recently, though, the entirety of Munchkin land was paying attention to Munchkin Town over Munchkinville because a Snark Snark had been seen in the area. Dorothy, of course, had never heard of a Snark Snark before and neither had Ozma but the Munchkin burgomeister had assured them one hadn't been seen in years.

"What does a Snark Snark look like?" Dorothy said, looking over her shoulder to see if one might be sneaking around where she wasn't looking. Toto was travelling with her as usual and he seemed rather bored with the entire proceeding.

"Nobody knows," Thaddeus Bumhug said, lifting up his candy cane scepter of office. It sounds silly until you realized Munchkin Town made candy for its livelihood. "Only I saw it many years ago, and it was invisible at that time. It is a terribly important creature and its' appearance should definitely be taken seriously by the royalty of the Emerald City. Would you like a candy cane Princess?" He handed one of his town's wares to Oot, which was white with green stripes.

"Hogwash! There's no such thing as a Snark Snark! Princess Dorothy, do not listen to my brother! He only wants to bring attention to his less prosperous village and it's less than tasty treats! He's been doing it for years!" Octavian Bumhug exclaimed as the visiting Mayor of Munchkinville pulled out a green with white striped candy cane. "Here, have some of my town's wares."

"Ridiculous! Just because you can't see a Snark Snark doesn't mean it can't be sighted! Just look at what it did to this poor fence!" Thaddeus Bumhug led Dorothy to the edge of the village, where he pointed to a rather large horse's pen whose wooden fence had been busted in half from the inside. A rather proud looking pony was sitting inside of the fence. Dorothy clutched Toto to her chest as she looked at the Mayor of Munchkin Town and asked, "Is it possible that your horse might be responsible for this instead of the Snark Snark?"

The Mayor of Munchkin Town looked incensed. "My horse responsible? Ridiculous!" The Mayor of Munckinville looked very pleased.

"Well it's possible..." Dorothy really didn't like making people cross.

"Harvey, are you responsible for breaking down my fence?" Thaddeus asked the horse. The horse spit out the hay he was chewing on. "Certainly not Mayor! Obviously it is the work of the Snark Snark you told me about earlier," The horse Harvey replied quite plainly.

"Oh dear." Dorothy said, hugging Toto towards her as the arguing between the two brothers commenced in earnest. The arguing was interrupted by the sound of rustling coming from the forest.

"GASP! It must be the Snark Snark! Your Highness, we have to get you to safety!" Thaddeus

The Wooing of Ozma

grabbed Dorothy by the arm and struggled to move the much larger girl, but Dorothy was trying to see who was emerging. She was surprised to see a young man about sixteen in very dirty church clothes, a giant toad wearing clothes, and Polychrome the Fairy.

"Don't be ridiculous. I know one of these people and she wouldn't hurt a fly." Dorothy shook away the Mayor's hand and turned to the newcomers even as a heavy rain shower began above them. Dorothy was taken aback because she could usually predict the weather fairly well, and she hadn't seen a cloud in the sky.

"Oh pardon me Miss. We were just passing through…." The young man said executing a rather comical bow to Dorothy as Polychrome hugged her. "Oh, I see you two know each other."

"Hello sir. Pleased to meet you. My name is Dorothy Gale." Dorothy offered her hand as the man walked up using his umbrella rather like a cane. The pair shook hands firmly and smiled at one another.

"A pleasure to meet you as well….ooops excuse my rudeness." The man then popped his umbrella open above them both "My name is Milo Starling and I have heard much about you Princess. I am a preacher, or would be one in any case."

Dorothy smiled to be out of the rain and looked at the man a bit more closely to take his measure "That's nice to hear, sir. I'm afraid we usually don't have much use for preachers around here, though. Everyone here is already naturally nice to each other."

"There are no sweeter words to be heard by a reverent I say unto thee. Does not the Good Book thus say it is not sacrifices and burnt offerings that is wanted, but life long service?" the man asked, smiling.

"I couldn't tell you actually." Dorothy looked at the heavy storm stewing about in the sky.

"I'm fairly certain it does." Milo nodded.

"Then why ask?" E. Bused murmured.

"Ah yes, this is my companion E. Bused, who is, despite being very well gifted as a Toad, not very fond of his shape. He was formerly a munchkin. He is, however, a very talented jester. If his vocals do need a bit of work." Milo nodded in his toad companion's direction.

"Oh dear, Lady Polychrome, E. Bused, would either of you like my place under the umbrella? It was very thoughtless of me not to offer it. Oh, excuse me," Milo said, seeing the two bickering Munchkin leaders who were scampering off following the onset of the rain.

"No I like the rain," Polychrome said dancing under its' dew. "It's just the awful thunder and lightning I hate."

"It's raining?" E. Bused looked up and put his webbed fingers to his waist. "Well I'll be. A toad's skin must be considerably different than a munchkin's…though I have no claws or teeth,'

This was something Dorothy found very odd to hear.

"- because I do not even feel the cold or droplets," the toad continued. "Please, by all means keep your umbrella, friend Milo for this rain is quite refreshing."

"I am very glad to hear of your enjoyment. Princess Dorothy, my friend and I are in a spot of trouble and we hope you might be able to help us with

The Wooing of Ozma

it. We have recently escaped a terrible kingdom and it is my desire to find a way to contact my home, which is most assuredly not Oz. It's not that your country is not beautiful, but I suspect there are those back in Kentucky who would be worried for me." Milo quickly added, "My friend on the other hand, wishes to be transformed from his present shape into something with a bit more dash than Toad."

"Perhaps a unicorn or a twenty foot tall giant with flaming red hair," E. Bused said. The Toad making gestures over his round, bald, and warty head.

Dorothy nodded as Toto barked. "I'm from Kansas originally. I'm sure Princess Ozma will be glad to help you out. She's always willing to help strangers in trouble. I know because I'm one of them...or was at least."

"This is the most joyous news we have had since we escaped our confines." Milo smiled before he noticed E. Bused pointing to the sky as seven claps of thunder and lightning followed in unison.

"Ummm, I don't think we quite escaped the confines," E. Bused said grimly.

Looking up, the group of travelers saw the terrible hissing-wings that loomed over the group. With eight claws extended on each of their eight fingered hands and their eyes glowing a terrible red they were among the fiercest of sights to be seen in Oz for many a year.

"WE MUST BRING THEM TO THE PRINCESSSSSSSS!" The Captain of the Guard screamed at the top of his lungs as he zoomed down upon the group. Truth be told, the number of hissing-wings would have rather plainly made short work of the group and taken them all to the dungeons of the

Charles Phipps

Princess Zoam but for the fact the Captain of the Guard wanted to taunt them some more with his claws and hissing wings before doing so. Something of which is a very cruel thing to do to a jester, little girl, rainbow fairy, and a young man who was just trying to get to church on time.

"Oh get away!" Dorothy called, clutching Toto even as the dog slipped out of her hands and bit the creature on the side of his leg. The Captain of the Guard knocked the dog down as Toto continued barking in the vain hope that it would scare the terrible bully off.

"Ha ha ha fear me, child." The Captain dipped its hands at Dorothy several times before a most unexpected thing happened…which by now everyone should expect in Oz.

"AWAY FROM HER WRETCH!" Milo shouted, and while being quite terrified (something you shouldn't fault a man for especially when he is dressed in filthy Sunday clothes and very cramped from being in a cold damp cage for a long period of time) he lifted up his umbrella and slapped it against the Captain's beak with all the force he had in his arm.

"OWWWWWWWWWWW!" The Hissing-wing commander cried, feeling his beak, even as he fell to the ground and ceased to flap his wings. The other Hissing-wings, seeing their leader struck by the cursed device, took to the sky and fled in abject terror.

"Wow," E. Bused said looking at the umbrella, which Milo himself was gazing at. An umbrella makes a poor weapon, you see, and Milo hadn't really expected it to drive them all off. Still he wasn't ungrateful that it had.

The Wooing of Ozma

"Oh no! No! No! No! No! You've struck me with….with…an umbrella!" The Captain cried, holding his snout. Now this is not entirely similar to the Nomes who fear chickens because they are destroyed by their eggs or the Wicked Witches who die if doused with water, for the Hissing Wing was undone for entirely different reason. Still, it is somewhat amusing that the fiercest of evils are often undone by such common things.

Dorothy was not sympathetic and picked up her dog. Having nothing to say to the Hissing-Wing, she merely glared at him.

"Well, I'm sorry if I hurt you sir, but you were doing something very wrong and I do not regret striking you to make you stop it," Milo said before quoting the Good Book again "The heavens are telling the glory of God, a marvelous display of craftsmanship…you were not making them very pleasant."

"No! No! I'm your slave forever now! Curses and double curses." The Hissing-Wing started to bang his head against the ground of Munchkin Town.

"Just because he hit you with an umbrella?" Dorothy asked, ignoring the rain about her as Toto barked.

"Yes! The Hissing-Wings have been enslaved ever since the time of Princess Zoam's father, but she, for all her magic and beauty, isn't very clever, and we could escape her easily if not for the weather-maker Igor." The Captain of the Guard started crying rather large tears that were the color of slime. "We're all afraid of him and his machines because he would seek

Charles Phipps

us out were we to escape and pelt us with such storms that we would never be able to fly again!"

Polychrome, despite having her dance interrupted by the terrifyingly ugly creatures, was sympathetic to someone who couldn't fly and started to pat the creature on the back of the head and embrace him.

"There, There," Polychrome said.

"And then how would we bash ourselves against the rocks, ground, and cliffs?" the Captain asked, and got somewhat less sympathy as the others around him exchanged uncomfortable looks. "However, long ago we heard the weather-maker Igor talking to the Princess about terrorizing the locals below with his storms and he boastfully but foolishly said that the only thing which could beat him was an umbrella. Taking note of this, we knew that whoever could wield such a weapon is more powerful than the weather-maker, and surely a more terrible master, so we vowed to serve whoever could strike us with one." The Captain of the Guard sniffled and wiped away his slimy tears. It was all quite logical to a hissing-wing's mind, you see, and one of the reasons hissing-wings are not commonly found in positions of leadership.

There was a moment of silence.

"You have got to be kidding me," Milo said.

"That is the silliest thing I've ever heard in my entire life, and I've heard some silly things," Dorothy laughed. In truth, she had, and I'm sure anyone who has read the chronicles before has an extensive knowledge of these silly things, and instead of repeating them, I kindly direct you to the writings of the previous Royal Historians.

The Wooing of Ozma

"Oh poor woeful creature." Polychrome hugged the Hissing-Wing one more time as E. Bused tried to console him as well.

"Worry not, Captain of the Guard, for while he wields a powerful weapon, the man Milo is not an unkindly master. He has not whipped me once for walking less than ten paces behind him or looking at him." E. Bused patted the Captain. It is unfortunate most inhabitants of Zo share the hissing-wings' logic.

"He's probably just waiting for a time that he can punish you for all of them at once." The Captain blew his nose on the jester's hat and then handed it back to him.

E. Bused calmly put the soiled object back on his thick toady head. (A Toad's reputation for tolerating muck is actually quite well deserved.) He looked at Milo. "You're not, are you?"

"No I am not," Milo said sincerely, as he blinked and squinted before cleaning his cracked glasses of the steam that had built up on them.

"Of that I am most grateful." E. Bused smiled.

Polychrome looked up. "I think this is a most terrible situation. Though I do love the showers, which bring me pleasure, the weather makers of Zo are terrible people who interfere with nature to ruin people's days. If they have followed us here, I am sure they mean to work mischief on all of Oz."

Dorothy nodded, "After seeing what this Princess and Igor have done to you already, I'm sure they are terrible too, and that Ozma will definitely want to know about it. Please come back with me to the Emerald City." Lifting Toto up she then called to the Munchkin mayors who had been rather fearfully hiding in their homes. Thaddeus and his brother having an aversion both to getting their clothes wet and terrifying monsters. "I'm sorry, Mayors, but something has come up and I think we'll need to be going now! Thanks for the peppermint! Keep a look out for the Snark Snark!" She waved her two candy canes, then handed one to E. Bused and the other to Polychrome because Dorothy, truth be told, didn't care much for peppermint at all.

Soon after, the Hissing-Wing got up and began to carefully follow the group as they walked down the Yellow Brick Road to their destiny in the Emerald City. Jumping puddles, singing, and enjoying the day, it was almost easy to ignore the terrible rain that was haunting Oz all around them.

The Wooing of Ozma
Chapter Four

The Wizard of Oz stared at the Lady Glinda as she poured through her magical Book of Records. The Wizard of Oz had on occasion entreated the Good Witch of the South to perhaps accompany him for the purposes of dinner, stargazing, or other semi-romantic activities, but the Grand Dame of Oz had never shown the slightest interest in his overtures. It was something he was sorry to say was true that she had no interest in her student as a potential partner. The Wizard admired the woman above all other things and it often frustrated him to no end that she was so much higher than he was.

'Well, be a good lad and be content with what you have. You're a good man and with her help you've become a very good wizard as well,' The Wizard smiled at the reflection of himself in a nearby mirror. "So Milady, have you had any indication of what might be causing our rather odious deluge?"

"Unfortunately the truth of the matter continues to elude me, Wizard. Wherever the people causing this storm are, they are not directly in Oz and thus my Book of Records will take a great deal of time examining to tell me much about them. However there are some very curious passages inside the tome that perhaps illuminate the cause..." Glinda looked up at the Wizard who nodded his head to indicate he was listening. Glinda usually only scanned her book for passages in Green ink and those that mentioned Oz which kept her from spending weeks reading a single

Charles Phipps

page since the book contained virtually everything happening in the world at once.

"Of course weather magic could be cast any number of places and sent on inward to Oz. It's entirely possible, for instance, for someone to simply chill the North Pole or other land and suddenly storms would appear all across the globe. So much is our ecology tied together that with a one degree heat variation a new ice age might begin whic..." the Wizard's train of thought was interrupted by Glinda's next words.

"...for instance here it says 'Milo Starling of the Land of Kentucky and E. Bused of the Land of Zo landed with Polychrome the fairy in the land of Oz and barely escaped the hissing-wings of Princess Zoam. They then joined up with Princess Dorothy of Oz to travel to the Emerald City.'" Glinda pointed out the passage, which was like Ancient Greek to the Wizard, or more precisely Latin, because he spoke Ancient Greek quite fluently thanks to a chance encounter with a Oxford historian on the road who'd traded lessons in it for balloon rides.

The Wizard tapped his chin with his front right fingers. "Hmmmm, most curious. I do believe I recall a Land of Zo while purusalling the Archives of the Emerald City. Isn't it a flying city that broke away from Oz some time ago?" Of course, there was no such word as purusalling, but it helped him to sound intelligent.

"Yes indeed. Prince Zo's home, a terrible place indeed. It still has the magic of Lurline's enchantment but as long as a ruler other than Ozma controls it, the book will not record its happenings as part of Oz. It is

The Wooing of Ozma

a dark day if the royal house of Oz has turned upon itself," Glinda shook her head sorrowfully and looked at the Wizard who simply nodded.

"Well it's just another invasion and I suspect with the Wishing Belt and our combined magical force we'll overcome this one just as surely as we've overcome everything else that has our way since the beginning of Oz," The Wizard puffed up his chest.

"Such as yourself," Glinda said looking at the Wizard with a more than slightly disapproving gaze. Above all, Glinda was a woman of propriety and despite the fact that the Wizard's rule was mostly a time of peace she had never quite forgiven him. His crimes of giving young Ozma up to Mombi and lying to the people for so many years tainted his later heroism in Glinda's mind. The thunder rattling outside her beautiful magical castle's doors didn't help her feelings toward him much either.

The Wizard of Oz immediately looked downcast before switching the subject. "In any case, I think there is a much greater matter to attend to Madame," the Wizard raised a finger. "One which you and I are uniquely able to comprehend above all others of Ozma's circle of confidents, collaborators, and friends!"

Glinda looked at the Wizard with a slightly cross expression before gesturing for her Lady of the Guard (which was so much more pleasant than mere "Captain"). The Lady of the Guard was needed to carry a message she wrote on a lovely scroll of vellum to the Princess Ozma. Glinda did not like any of her pretty uniformed guards to get themselves wet and messed up in this terrible weather but her swans could hardly fly in this kind of rain. If not for the Red Wagon she'd still be at the Emerald City.

"My dear Glinda, I do believe that we need to find a suitable companion for the Lady Ozma to ring in the new…whatever year it is presently," the Wizard pulled out his pocket watch and tapped it. Unfortunately, the device had not been wound properly and the Oz year was distinctly different from the standard calendar of the United States and Europe.

The Lady of the Guard spun around to listen to the conversation even as she exited the room but Glinda with a wave of her wand shut the doors in front of her. Glinda didn't want her army of young women to hear any gossip regarding the monarch of Oz. "You cannot be serious Oscar."

The Wizard of Oz chuckled to himself and cracked his knuckles "Why my dear, there is nothing I have ever been more serious about in my life."

"The Princess of Oz does not require a mate!" Glinda lowered her wand and put it to one side, highly annoyed.

"Mate? Pishaw! You make it sound so primitive Glinda, barbaric even. I've been in traveling shows my entire life out of Oz and I can tell you in that time I've learned to recognize a few things about my audience and that includes when a girl is ready to get star-crossed!" The Wizard of Oz smiled as he cast open the shutters into the rainy night. "Ozma is on the cusp of womanhood, Glinda, and such a day should be filled with suitors and parties and flirtations and other things to make her life more enjoyable!"

The twinkle in the eye of the Wizard almost made the Good Witch of the South ill. "Perhaps you are forgetting this, Wizard, but Princess Ozma is a fairy, and as such is always going to be 'on the cusp of womanhood' and never a woman entirely. Furthermore I am quite of the opinion that there is no spouse in all of Oz and beyond which could possibly be a suitable husband for her."

"Glinda you think too harshly. Certainly faeries age slower than mortals and in Oz one does not need age at all, but she certainly can if she so wishes. Suitors are made Glinda, not born, and any man who truly loves Ozma will shape himself into the object of her desire as she is his. This imaginary suitor I think just needs a little push once we've found the right candidate." The Wizard smiled impishly as Glinda shook her head 'no' a dozen times.

The Wizard sighed at Glinda's final pronouncement of "No."

"Mark my words, Glinda, if you do not wade in the river with me to steer the tide of emotion, then by Heavens the river will hit it's target far sooner and uncontrollably." It wasn't a metaphor that made much sense but it was a memorable one Oscar thought.

Oscar Zoroaster Phadrig Issac Norman Henkle Emmanuel Ambroise Diggs wasn't aware just how right he would be in his pronouncement.

***

Dorothy Gale, Toto, Polychrome, Milo Starling, the former Captain of Zoam's guard (whose name was Raspy) and E. Bused arrived at the Emerald City when the Moon was reaching its crest. Or at least it would be reaching it's crest if they could see it through the endless storm clouds that covered every inch of Oz's

Charles Phipps

sky. Once they reached the gates of the magnificent metropolis, however, the newcomers were surprised to discover their reception was remarkably cold.

"G..gg..gg…goo…dd…even…nn..nnn…nnn…ning Miss Dor…Dor…Dor…" the Soldier with the Green Whiskers tried to speak out. Even dressed in a heavy emerald raincoat, his teeth were chattering. Omby Amby's breath was visible even in the freezing drizzle pouring down. Dorothy herself had a bit of a chill despite that she was spared the worst of it by the umbrella over her head.

"Oh heavens, Omby Amby you look awful! You should head in immediately and get yourself some nice cocoa before you catch pneumonia," Dorothy said, wondering if anyone really got sick in Oz. For the life of her, Dorothy couldn't remember anyone suffering the chills, measles, or anything else during her stay. Even if he couldn't get sick the Soldier looked very uncomfortable anyway.

"C…C…ca…caa…ca…nt leave my post," he said with the last word sneezing out of his nostrils.

"I say, good man. You should have a doctor look you over." Milo looked him over.

Polychrome then stepped forward and smiled. "Wait, worry not, I think I can help you! I can enchant your raincoat to keep you warm and dry even through the worst of weather conditions."

"Mu…Mu…muc…" Omby Amby then sneezed heavily on the entire group, which caused Toto to start to sniffle.

"I say, do learn to cover your mouth when you do that." Milo reached in his pockets and pulled out some

The Wooing of Ozma

tissues. He always kept some in his Sunday best for these sort of occasions.

"Oh no…" Dorothy clutched Toto tightly to her chest. Her dog getting sick was something Dorothy just could not abide.

"S…So…So…*HONK*," the Soldier with Green Whiskers gratefully accepted the tissues as Polychrome made the water dripping off his emerald coat glimmer and glow. Before long, the Soldier appeared much more comfortable. His beard was still completely soaked, and that was probably the reason he had caught such a chill despite having a raincoat on, but even that glowed a bit and was soon warmed. Once the magic was done Omby Amby was dry as a bone and unaffected by the rain as it continued to pour down. "Thank you Princess Dorothy! Lady Polychrome! Your efforts in securing the sanctity of the Emerald City are welcomed as always!" The Soldier then gave a salute which caused everyone to imitate him almost automatically before he began their escort into the city.

"I don't mean to be a pest, but that seems like an awful waste of magic there. I mean, you're the Princess. Why not simply order the man into someplace warm? It's not like one guard is going to do much good against the combined armies of Princess Zoam either," E. Bused murmured with a webbed hand over his mouth into Dorothy's ear.

"Oh things just aren't done that way here!" Dorothy said, shocked.

The Emerald City had mostly gone to bed. Only a few lights were visible inside the city. At night, in this rain, the wondrous city looked practically deserted and cold. It was a rather sharp contrast to the soft twinkling home that Dorothy had always known it to be even in the darkest night. Still, she wasn't paying attention to such things right now since Toto had caught a cold and was sneezing up a fit.

"I must say I've never met a proper princess before," Milo said, walking down the orange roads of the city. Even completely dark he was impressed by the beautiful architecture and wonderful gem work that was nothing like the dark spires of the Obsidian palace or more preferably, his home town in Kentucky.

"You met Princess Zoam...AH! Hehe," E. Bused said to his companion and got the joke perhaps before some people reading this chronicle did. Just for the readers to note, even though Princess Zoam perhaps deserves to be mocked a bit, it really wasn't very nice of Milo to make such a comment. However we'll forgive him because she actually isn't a proper princess. Dorothy was also princess indeed but Milo and she had become such good friends in their short time he felt hard pressed to call her a 'proper' Princess. Dorothy didn't seem to much care for her title anyways and it had made her much more comfortable just to be called by her name.

The Emerald Palace wasn't much more active than the city as the rain had forced those people not staying away to patch up the leaks and clean out the buckets to an early bed. Ozma week's festivities had also tired out a goodly portion of the guests. Still, the throne room of Oz was quite active, even at this time of night, with Jellia trying out the throne of Princess Ozma. Jellia liked to do this when said person was preparing for bed, along with trying out her crown and scepter. The

The Wooing of Ozma

Cowardly Lion was sleeping at the foot of the throne on a rug woven specially for him by the Gillikens. When the strange party from Munchkinland stepped in, it was quite a scene. E. Bused leapt on Milo's back at the sight of the Cowardly Lion, Dorothy curtsied and Milo bowed, dropping the poor toad man on the ground and waking up the lion.

"Visitors Your Highness!" Omby Amby said at the top of his lungs as the Lion put his paws to his ears. It's a wise bit of advice to never wake a sleeping lion, even one as congenial as the Cowardly Lion.

"Hail Your Highness Princess Ozma," Milo said with a smile before he became acutely conscious of Dorothy's embarrassment.

"Good evening Noble Knight. I indeed am Princess Ozma and I welcome you to my kingdom. You must greatly wearied from your travels and I…" Jellia began before she received a rather firm "Hush" from Dorothy.

"I was just curtseying to be polite," Dorothy said. "This is Jellia Jamb, one of Ozma's closest friends."

"I was…well my eyelashes are drooping and I only saw your bow," Omby Amby said, shaking his head, mortified.

"I found these nice travelers trapped on top of a flying island and decided with my father to bring them to Oz. I hope that's alright, since Glinda went to all the trouble about making Oz invisible to outsiders, but it seems to me that she'd rather I take them here than leave them up there." Polychrome declared. The Sky Fairy was multicolored and very beautiful, illuminating the room in a variety of colors despite the low light. "Unfortunately, the cloud I brought them here from seems to have icky well followed us."

"Your Lion is the…C…Cowardly one right?" E. Bused asked crawling up Milo's leg. The toad man then let out a rather heavy "Boo!" in hopes of scaring the Lion off. When the cowardly lion did not move E. Bused asked, "…A…Arn't you terrified?"

"Yes, don't do that again or I shall have to eat you to end my terror," The Cowardly Lion said, licking his paws.

Milo, acutely conscious of the fact he might be responsible for bringing this rather depressing sleet on the lovely countryside, and that the conversation was taking an ugly turn coughed into his hand and said simply, "Pardon me Madame Jamb…"

"Jellia, please," Jellia smiled.

"You're very sweet," Milo said, oddly feeling like he'd committed a mortal sin for some reason. Puns were clearly spoken of against in the Good Book, and if they weren't they should have been. "If it is alright, I would like to speak to your reigning monarch Princess Ozma regarding a matter of the utmost importance to your kingdom."

Dorothy nodded in assent as both Amby and the Cowardly Lion suddenly stood erect.

"Are you sure you want to speak to her now? You look like you walked out of a dungeon into a rainstorm wearing your Sunday best," Jellia noted, looking at the man's clothing.

Milo looked down at his soiled clothes with a sigh. Raising up his umbrella he wagged it a bit in the air to clean off the rain. Unfortunately for Miss Jamb, this accidentally covered her in some water droplets "Oops.

The Wooing of Ozma

Errr...I commend you on your remarkable powers of observation. Nevertheless, I would like to speak to your ruler immediately."

Dorothy nodded, still extremely shaken up by her experience with the hissing-wing, and not particularly consoled by having the creature standing next to her less than a foot away. "Best to do as he says Jellia. There's some very bad people responsible for this awful rain. I'm pretty sure if it doesn't stop it may even ruin Uncle Henri's newest crop. Oh dear, does anyone know someone who could help Toto? He's caught a dreadful cold!"

"Come sit him by my fur so that he can be warm," the Cowardly Lion said. Dorothy did so and the Lion wrapped Toto in his mane.

"Well, it does sound important. So I suppose you can interrupt the Princess as she's preparing for sleep. Go up the stairs to your right to the highest emerald tower and you're sure to find Ozma. Her doors are the ones marked with the O with the Z inside it." Jellia gestured to the stairs. Milo nodded and began his trek up the stairs.

"Shall I accompany you Masssssssster?" Raspy the Hissing-Wing asked.

"Actually, why don't I show you a few new dance steps?" Polychrome grabbed the monster by the arms and began to lead him in a rainbow waltz before he could follow the young man. Polychrome thought it might be nice to make a good impression on Ozma with her visitors and while the monarch of Oz's capacity to love oddities was legendary, she wasn't sure how the ruler of Oz would react to the crash prone Raspy.

Charles Phipps

Milo gulped as he stood before the princess's forbidding doors. To say that the young man was nervous right now was an understatement. To be cool and collected to a Princess when she has kept you a prisoner and your only thought was escape was one thing (not to mention adjusting to fact magic was real). To keep one's cool while trying to visit a friend, and entreat her help when you knew her to be just, good, and beautiful was something else entirely. Milo noticed there was a strange similarity to the symbol on the door and the Princess of Zoam's crown but put it out of his mind. Such a coincidence was the least thing he was to encounter in such a place as this, he expected.

"I suppose I should bow," Milo thought. The polite movement was a very good ice -breaker in conversations. Given she was a princess, Milo actually got so low his forehead was touching the floor. As he lifted his hand to knock on the bottom of the door, Milo heard the door creak open. Clearing his throat to introduce himself to the supreme ruler of Oz, Milo opened his mouth to speak. It was then that he felt a rather unpleasant sensation of being stepped on. Ozma the Princess of Oz had walked out of her room and tripped completely over the unexpected obstacle in her path, sending her head over his heels.

***

Princess Zoam looked at the gigantic collection of Quadlings, Gillikens, Munckins, China people, Skeezers, Flatheads, Giants, Nomes, Loons, Stuffed bears, Flying Monkeys, Cuttinclips, and virtually every other conceivable character that has been recorded in

The Wooing of Ozma

the previous chronicles of the Royal Historians. So many that, once again, an accurate summary would take a great deal of space from this book so I will simply say the prisoners of Zoam were many. The menagerie of the Supreme Ruler of Zo was kept in chains forged from Zonium, a magical metal that was only found in clouds and bound in spells that made them both passive and extremely flattering to the queen. It was all in all a dreary sight, this Dungeon.

"I will release the first person who gives me the correct answer to my questions," Princess Zoam said as she lifted up her wand "Where is the location of the Emerald City?"

The dungeon was full of hundreds of answers which occasionally were not correct. Ozma, despite many years on the throne, was still not universally known among her subjects. The monsters Princess Zoam had sent had also simply picked the first of every race they found to bring to her as opposed to scholars or others who might know better. Still the first answer Princess Zoam received was "In the center of Oz.", and Princess Zoam was true to her word. Ordering her guards to take the young Gilliken lad who had said them and toss him from the top of Zo they did so. As immensely evil as that action may seem to you or me, it was actually for the young man's benefit because since no one can die in the Oz. The young prisoner was simply in for a long period of recovery (once he hit the ground) and more importantly, he was free. Still it was odd how answers to Princess Zoam's other questions were less than forthcoming after his 'release'.

Charles Phipps

"Perhaps, Your Gracefulness, you should not have released him in front of the other prisoners," Igor said, walking up behind the woman whom he willingly served out of love. It was not a healthy love like a father for his daughter, or a friend for a friend, or even a man for a wife but an all-consuming obsession that he never let Zoam have the slightest hint of. In truth, he was more afraid of her rejecting him than he was living with her never knowing there was something to reject.

"Oh bah! They will answer me or I will do with them what I did to those incompetent guards who couldn't retrieve for me my lost pets." Zoam looked at the group of piglets who were squealing in a nearby corner. The once feared hissing-wings were now little more than ornery, messy, smelly, and greedy pups which meant they hadn't changed much in personality but they had changed considerably in size and shape.

"Perhaps we should save some of our soldiery for the actual invasion of Oz, Your Mercilessness." Igor Lackey looked down at piglets.

"I have already interrogated many of the inhabitants of Oz and learned much. There will be no need for invasion of Oz because not only is there a Princess Ozma ruling the land of Oz but I have discovered that I resemble her so strongly that everyone initially took me for her. I have also learned that a terrible desert continues to surround Oz that will turn to dust anyone who attempts to cross it on foot. Thus once I have assumed command of the throne of Oz, we will flood the entire land so that everyone and everything in Oz is poured out into their Deadly Desert and annihilated!" Zoam smiled a truly diabolical grin.

The Wooing of Ozma

Igor put his face in his hands. "Your Terribly Wrathfulness, there isn't much point in conquering a land if you're just going to completely destroy it, is there?"

Princess Zoam blinked as that thought occurred to her for the first time. "I knew that. I was testing you."

"Of course, Your Cleverness." Igor bowed his head low before his ruler.

"Prepare the Sleep Lillies for this so called Princess Ozma. I will meet with my cousin down below in her palace and ask her to surrender her kingdom to me peacefully. If she does not then….I will take her place and destroy her lands." Zoam smiled again as she dreamed of the flooded and destroyed Oz that she would rule.

"Your Strangely Compelling Vileness, didn't we just agree that it would be better if you replaced her NOT to dest…" Igor stopped in mid-sentence realizing that the Princess was no longer listening to him again. "Forget it. As you wish, You're In Need of Protectioness," he said the last title under his breath as he went back to his work creating rainstorms.

Chapter Five

Ozma was completely at home in the Royal Apartments of Oz. Her Magic Picture, her collection of three thousand gowns (each more beautiful than the last), her personal library with every book by every Ozzite ever written and quite a few tomes from the outside world, and her spell shop where she studied her magic were all known to her by heart. In other words it was not the sort of place where she was likely to suddenly trip and fall. Frankly speaking, it was very much unlike her to be so clumsy because clumsy isn't very royal.

"Oh pardon me madam…errr…are you Princess Ozma? I was leaning over to pick up an emerald which had fallen off your door…I was told to speak with you about…some things," a voice spoke beneath the Princess's legs.

With a little bit of effort she rolled off of the man and looked at him. Ozma gazed at his features and took them in very clearly. He was about a year older than Ozma appeared to be and there was kindness in his look but also a certain embarrassment that most likely had to do with the fact he had just tripped her royal personage. Ozma noticed that he was also looking at her in a way that made her feel quite strange and likely to blush, which she rarely did.

"Yes I am indeed, sir," Ozma rose. "That's strange, I don't see an emerald anywhere or missing off my door." Ozma turned the conversation back to his reported reason for tripping her high personage. The stranger had arrived at her door at a very fortuitous

The Wooing of Ozma

moment. A previous chronicle recorded a time when Princess peered at her magic picture to see her true love and she saw the door where he now stood…an event that only occurred a moment or two ago Oz-time speaking. The man did not immediately answer and Ozma waved her hand in front of his eyes until he got ahold of himself again. To her pleasure, Ozma realized that he had been staring at her and had been positively dumbstruck.

"Oh sorry, pardon me milady." the man got up and dusted himself off as Ozma took note that the poor fellow was slightly embarrased. He looked like he'd been wearing in his Sunday clothes before going through a dungeon, descending on a rainbow, trekking through the forest, then getting caught in a rainstorm. "In truth milady, there was no missing emerald and I committed a grave error upon your personage by telling…an untruth…I am deeply sorry and take the blame it on a weak soul that could not bear even the slightest bit of your ire."

Ozma blinked, wondering what strange country this man must come from that lies are preferable to the truth when speaking to someone. "Your apology is accepted though please…" Ozma noticed the man was kissing her hand and was on his knees now; it gave her a very odd feeling of giddiness. "Do not lie again…"

"Never again, Milady. I thank you for your forgiveness. Lady, with all my heart I thank you. I will sing your praises before the armies of angels in heaven." the man bowed his head before Ozma. "My name is Milo Starling, and it is with a deep and sad heart that I do however bring grim tidings."

Ozma gripped her wand slightly at the compliments before she became acutely conscious she was in her nightgown. Making a wave of sparkling magic Ozma was suddenly dressed in a lovely blue sequined dress. Ozma bed crown was replaced with her courtly crown and otherwise looked much more queenly. "I am very grateful you are willing to speak so kindly of me to such august personages and also glad to have another person in Oz who can sing. Strangely, most do not have the talent but that does not stop them. Pray tell, are you another traveler from the Americas to my kingdom? Perhaps fair Kansas?"

"Ah no, milady, I am from Kentucky which is under the same King we call the President but a different region of the realm," Milo adjusted his tie. Milo was acutely he couldn't sing a note and it was far far too soon to be breaking a promise to such an angel on Earth to never lie.

"Ah, and what is the difference between this Kansas and Kentucky?" Ozma asked. Oz had been invaded several times before, and it was always less interesting to deal with that than learning about the homelands of new arrivals in Oz. It had been entirely Glinda's suggestion they isolate Oz and Ozma bitterly regretted it. Ozma was half human herself and wanted to know as much of the mortal lands as she could.

"Mostly, Milady Wondrous, it is like Kansas, only with more hills and blue grass, though it's not blue..." Milo stopped in mid sentence to think about that.

"It sounds most intriguing, Sir Starling." It was an appropriate name for the man who had just flown the coop, as it appeared. Her words had the intended effect and his cheeks flushed bright red at the even slightest

The Wooing of Ozma

bit of praise that she gave him…a common enough affliction of Ozites, but oddly Ozma felt particularly pleased about this effect on her new friend.

"Indeed, and I fear, milady, that as much as I wish to tell you these things, that there is much to be done. The evil Princess Zoam, who is about as evil as one can be to a person who doesn't really believe in evil but she comes darn close to convincing him, has assembled a terrible army in the sky where her kingdom lays and her equally vile assistant Igor has a weather machine which allows her to perhaps be causing this very storm outside." Milo told her what he knew in a very rapid and, to anyone but Ozma, extremely confusing tone. Not to mention in an extremely large run-on sentence.

"I see. You realize that was a very large run on sentence, correct?" Ozma said lifting her wand and going over the information.

"I heard it all, Lady, while her prisoner. Yes I also note it was an extremely large run on sentence. A terrible situation, but one I was willing to deal with without too much complaint. The information she provided will hopefully allow me to prevent a great evil," Princess Zoam, for all of her wickedness, was quite the gossip to her caged prisoner. It was almost as if nature was doing its best to compensate for her small heart by giving her a big mouth. Personally, Milo had been too amazed by his situation for the days he'd been kept prisoner to really bother to be horrified or scared of it. Incurable curiosity was occasionally useful.

"Indeed. What does this Princess Zoam look like?" Ozma asked, looking at Milo. Perhaps she could be approached as fellow royalty and convinced to abandon her quest. If this Princess Zoam would not listen to reason and while many did whom Ozma talked to, few followed the advice she gave, then there was always the Wishing Belt to resolve matters.

It was as if Milo looked upon Ozma in an entirely different light and was embarrassed by what he saw. Milo was one of those rare people who saw a person by their personality and subtle signs before obvious ones. "Milady, as strange as it may seem to you she resembles you a great deal you…in fact you could be twins."

Ozma, descending the stairs to join her court and figure out a way to deal with this terrible threat stopped cold. Whatever she had been expecting it had most certainly not been that particular revelation. Evil was a hideous thing and she had never had such associated with her face before. "She does, truly?"

"Her face, hair, and body are identical, Lady, yet verily, I say unto you that no person could stand in your presence and make the mistake of confusing you for long should they know. Where your face is kindly and sweet hers only holds ambition and cruelty. You walk like a fairy princess…" Milo was stopped by the realization she was a fairy princess. "And she…well her walk is more like a predator's."

"Do not doubt for a moment if you are to stay in Oz for any length of time, Traveler Starling, that not all faeries are good and kind I fear." Ozma lowered her head and went through the possibilities of what the source of her doppleganger could be. Was Zoam a witch who had enchanted herself to look like her? Was this Zoam a twin created from her shadow…no, that

The Wooing of Ozma

was there on the ground where it always was. The most hideous thought was that she was perhaps a relative but Ozma forced that aside. The idea that her line would contain someone horrid was shocking on a deeply personal level to her. Lineage was as important as deed to a fairy, for the sins of a father were always lain on their children among the fey…always.

Milo was silent to the ruler of Oz because he wished truly to say something bold like 'If you are present Princess then I shall never leave Oz again," but you must realize that Milo Starling was a plain boy from Kentucky, if a bit polite and gentlemanly, even among normal plain boys who are already the most polite and gentlemanly of them all. Being so plain and gentlemanly, he did not have the courage to speak what was, as you might already guess, was plain as the nose on his face to us: Milo had fallen in love with Princess Ozma at first sight. "I hope to stay your majesty," he blurted out instead.

Ozma turned her attention to Milo who looked at her with such eyes that she felt almost underdressed. Ozma knew on some level fate would play a part in making a place for him in her life but Ozma never rushed fate, Ozma didn't rush fate ven if she felt strangely small under his gaze. Ozma did not particularly believe in destiny because she preferred to think of things as products of her own decisions.

"I'm glad of that," Ozma said. She thought for a moment about the situation. It was shocking for a fairy but she did not want to let the young mortal know of such things or hold them against her. So resolved, she said, "Let me say that you are welcome in my kingdom as long as you desire for as long as I rule. I insist the royal tailors make for you new clothes to replace your old, gold rimmed frames and emeralds to replace your glasses, and the royal bath for well…no offense intended…" Ozma didn't know how to broach the subject, truly, to the man who seemed so genuinely nice. The Royal Tailors had slept all afternoon and were thus fully awake at this time of night; it wouldn't be proper to mention the reason had been a rather large amount of wine.

Milo took one moment to sniff his Sunday clothes' sleeve. "Say no more. I shall avail myself to them."

"I shall thus prepare my court to deal with the person…who bears my reflection." Ozma thought about this again and gave a brief shudder at the stain that this made on Oz's history. No good had ever come of a family of the fey making war upon itself, and when the wicked among the fey joined against the good only suffering could emerge. The ancient conflict between the Courts of the Seelie and Unseelie fey were not so distant a memory. As Milo continued on his way out Ozma looked at him and said one last thing, "Do hurry I would like very much to discuss your homeland." which was a true though she felt a bit forward. Ozma wanted to talk to him though more than anything.

"I look greatly forward to it…Your Highness." The preacher to be made a very swift exit for he was mortally terrified of souring whatever good impression he might of made. It is a terrible thing to feel that you are unworthy of what (among both faeries and men) is the most cherished of emotions, but you'll again forgive this flawed mortal for feeling his inadequacy in spades. In his heart he made a private vow to become

The Wooing of Ozma

worthy of Princess Ozma's heart and win her love somehow, even if he had to die trying (and he might well with such a mindset). It was not just Princess Ozma who had fallen head over heals at first sight after all.

***

Sometime later, Princess Ozma in her royal throne room sometime later found herself unable to concentrate on her royal duties. Her mind was on matters pertaining to them, but were most sincerely not what was being talked about. Her mind kept wandering back to her conversation with Jellia, what she'd seen in the Magic Picture, and the young visitor who brought news of a dire threat to Oz.

'Oh dear me,' Ozma shook her head in thought.

Her throne room was mostly empty, and only a few of her closest associates were there. First was her chamberlain (and maid) Jellia, who was emptying buckets of the water leaking down into the room. To explain how a palace made of emeralds now suddenly had holes leaking water would require another book to tell, you about so please accept that the throne room was both wet and mucky. Her closest friend Dorothy was at her throne's side looking at her oddly, and Glinda's Lady of the Guard, Esmerelda Cinderwhite, was standing before her waiting for an answer to the letter Glinda had sent. The letter confirming Ozma's relationship to Zoam rested unfolded on the Princess's lap.

"Shall I send a reply back to the Good Witch of the South Your Highness?" Esmerelda Cinderwhite, the Lady of the Guard, asked.

Charles Phipps

"Hmmm?" Ozma looked up. "I don't know what to say, actually. I can't believe though that someone who shares the same blood of the royal family of Oz can be as evil as she seems. It must be a mistake of some kind." Ozma then handed the letter to Jellia to put in the royal archives, which she had found out only last week was the rubbish bin.

"Don't worry, Ozma, even a good tree occasionally gives bad apples. Ain't nothing to be ashamed of," Dorothy consoled her best friend by patting her on the arm.

Ozma took Dorothy's hand and squeezed it. "Thank you, Dorothy. I have resolved what my next course of action shall be. I must speak with she who rules over the land that was once part of Oz and, fate willing, shall be again. I just have to control my feelings in the matter…"

"And stop her from making it rain," Jellia said, lifting up four buckets. She carried two her hands, one with her teeth, and one with her left leg as she poured them out the throne room window. Finishing one by one, she put them back in place to catch more dripping water. It was quite a change from her normal duty, which was usually light dusting.

Ozma actually smiled at Jellia's joke as she nodded. "I can assure you that is also part of my goal." Many of Ozma's friends and associates were also staying in the palace, because the flooding was so bad in some parts of Oz that their homes had been completely destroyed or submerged. "Hmmm, Lady Cinderwhite, would you please carry this message back through the…" Ozma felt suddenly very guilty

The Wooing of Ozma

for putting the young maiden in Glinda's service back on the road, "back to Glinda come the morning?"

Ozma pulled out a sheet of paper and wrote with a dodo feather her response:

"Dearest Glinda-
As shocking as it may sound that the unseelie runs strong in my cousin, I am grateful that you placed this knowledge in my possession," Ozma thought about the next words and then wrote "Also, please send me any information about the traveler from America, if you can find any regarding him."

Jellia, looking over Ozma's shoulder, said, "Hmmm, you want to know about the traveler from America? You suspect him of being an evil wizard, a long lost prince of some foreign country, or do you just think he's cuuttttee?" Jellia smiled at Ozma.

The Princess was suddenly very cross with her chamberlain and said in perhaps too sharp of a tone, "That, Jellia, is a personal matter, and one that I do not care to discuss If I did care to discuss it, perhaps I would not..." Ozma looked at Jellia and realized what a perfectly droll response that was.

Dorothy blinked at Ozma with a strange cast to her face for a moment. "You mean that nice young man that Polychrome rescued? Why Ozma, I do believe you've got an eye on a boy," Dorothy said, with a positively delicious grin. The situation was extremely amusing for Dorothy, who was old enough in body to understand such things, but young enough to enjoy adult's discomfort with such.

Charles Phipps

"Dorothy, I'm the ruler of Oz, and I have said I would never marry nor fall in love. There are many reasons for this, even though I know you cannot understand them. If I marry, then the person shall never be able to live anywhere else but Oz, and though I hope for you and your family to stay here forever Dorothy, the choice will be taken away from him forever. He will never be my equal in marriage because this is my kingdom and I would not ask anyone to stand under me instead of at my side. Worse, Dorothy, faeries who loved mortals have never had anything but heartache throughout our history, and usually it is the mortal who suffers the most." Ozma despaired, having had all of these objections, and many more, running through her mind. "This is all even presuming that I have anything more than a fascination for this young man, let alone love him, or that he even feels the same way!"

"Pardon me Your Majesty, but my grandparents on both my sides were mortals and faeries both. If you don't mind my intruding," Esmerelda Cinderwhite said as she felt the red suspenders on her bright blue uniform slacks. "Thus, it means I am a full-blooded fairy, but both my parents are mortals who merely share the blood. I do not know when I shall take a husband and I do not intend to look because I am certain such a man as that I require: one willing to cook, clean, and raise children without fuss will come to me in time. I am sure he will be a mortal as no fairy would ever dip so low."

Ozma nodded at the woman. "I am sure such an oddity, if anywhere, will be found in Oz. Though you might ask General Jinjur about such. For she has

The Wooing of Ozma

already made certain her husband fills those duties quite nicely."

"Sadly, it would sadly be my luck, Your Highness, that the General of the Revolt would find the one I seek before me," Esmerelda said sulkily. "But I am very good at training, so I will set myself to a new task should I find who I am NOW quite certainly looking for."

Jellia found this all very amusing. "You're more afraid of nothing than the Cowardly Lion, Princess. The reasons fairy relationships so crumble is because they usually involve the very selfish and wicked among your people, Ozma. I would know because I've had to deal with quite a few while you're away saving Oz all the time." Jellia waved the buckets in her hand around like a saber and splashed the Lady of the Guard quite full in the face with their contents. "Oops." Jellia blinked.

The Lady of the Guard glared at Jellia before squeezing her woolen hat to dry it. Ozma and Dorothy were far too polite to burst out laughing at this, so they just smiled slightly and looked concerned. Jellia was already trying in vain to clean the Lady of the Guard's shirt with a wet sponge.

"Ozma, it's just ridiculous to believe he wouldn't love you back," Dorothy said. "Everyone loves you and I dare you to find any who doesn't."

Princess Ozma smiled at Dorothy for a moment then said, "Tell that to Princess Zoam." For all of the efforts of the group of young women to convince their sovereign, Ozma remained unconvinced love could truly be hers, even faced with all the evidence to the contrary.

Charles Phipps

***

Igor Lackey paced about the top floor of his tower. The tower was directly across from the palace of Zoam in the Obsidian City of Zo. It was a large craggy thing that twisted and turned in circles held only up by magic. Igor's home away from home was also covered in large sections of piping that funneled water, poisons, and terrible noxious fumes to and from the building as smokestacks poured out black choking fog from morning 'til night 'til morning again. All in all, it was type of place that perfectly resembled his personality.

"Hmmmm perhaps this. Yes." The alchemist said. He needed this refuge away from the palace to conduct his experiments. If the extent of his failures to create truly brilliant innovations were ever known to Zoam, then surely he would be kicked off from the top of his tower to the world below. Worse, he'd never see Zo or its beautiful ruler again. Currently the mad scientist was dressed in his laboratory coat and goggles amidst his electrical chargers, bottles, and doodads for the preparation of a very special a potion.

"A pinch of this and a pinch of that...yes!" Igor lifted up the concoction and poured it on a section of the sickly lillies which had been gathered up in an ugly bouquet for Princess Ozma. When the potion touched the flowers they suddenly brightened and turned into vibrant beautiful poppies.

"Perfect." Igor smiled. The Sleeping Lilies were now as lovely as their cousins in appearance.

"You waste much for your mistress. Why not simply overthrow her and take the throne for yourself?

The Wooing of Ozma

I'm sure many lovely maidens would love you much more than she loves you," said a voice both twisted and harsh came from the shadows. Igor looked at the figure that crept from them with a bit of a sour frown. Harpies were terrible creatures who had the face and arms of women but the body and claws of hawks. Why they were called harpies is unknown, but Professor Wogglebug often speculated that it was because harps are involved in classical music and most people hate it as much as they do the flying monsters.

"Just who I wanted to see, Agatha. I need you to take over the security of the Land of Zo. I've begun enchanting the island to strengthen its defenses ten fold with every magic I know, but without Raspy to be our captain of the guard, the army is without leadership." Igor Lackey did not even dignify the harpie's words with a comment.

"Ha! You presume too much of the children of Oz! It has been many years since we dwelled there, but the harpies remember what it was like. Powerful witches could rule and command just as easily as any fairy lords restrained by love. You'd do well to act like your grandmother the Wicked Witch." Agatha smiled, puckering her lips as her withered face loomed toward Igor. "Have you no kiss for your mother?"

Igor sucked in his chest and walked over to pressing his lips quickly on his mother's. He walked quickly to the other side of the lab with a fast walk. Harpies, in addition to their great strength, could also breathe fire and turn into beautiful women for a short time. Igor's father had been the son of the Wicked Witch of the West but banished by Glinda with his wife into the sky. Eventually they had found Zo, which provided them with the evil they needed yet also the familiarity of Oz.

'In hopes we might eventually return,' Igor thought. The infant Igor had been raised as a ward of King Zo but his mother had always drilled in him a desire for revenge. His father had possessed similar ambitions before King Zo had pushed him off Zo into the sea for saying his new hat was ugly. Igor often wondered what had happened to the old man because as an Ozite, he could never die. Likely Evile Lackey was still working mischief on the bottom of the ocean floor.

"Remember, mother, that we did not come to Zo because we liked it," Igor reminded her gently they had been driven out. "Glinda had powerful magic even when Pastoria was driven away, and she now has many new allies from what I understand. One a great witch named Dorothy who slew both my grandmother and her sister! I do not want to destroy Zo in a futile attempt at justice." Igor, of course, had no compunctions about destroying Oz but as dark, smelly, dismal, and ugly as Zo was, it was home and Zoam's only kingdom. Best to make sure to tread carefully before hitting, lest the Ozlanders hit back.

"Zo will not matter once we have stolen the powers of Glinda and the other Good Witch. They will trade anything for their Princess once this ridiculous plan of your lover's fails," the old crone cackled at Igor's discomfort, and she smiled a fangy grin. "In the meantime, I will tell your sisters, my daughters, and my grandchildren of my new status as leader of the Army of Zo and we will prepare for…attack…" the

The Wooing of Ozma

word caught in her throat and nearly sent Agatha into peels of laughter, "from the Ozites."

Igor cut his mother off with his next words "Do so, and do so now."

Charles Phipps

Chapter Six

Once suitably cleaned up from his trials, Milo T. Starling (T standing for Trustworthy), lay on a couch in the far corner of the royal apartments. Milo was bedecked in his new rainments, which had the singular uniqueness in Oz as to be exactly the same as his other pair of clothes, except cleaner. Milo was staring at the ceiling clutching his seven new umbrellas, all of them having been made at the insistence of the Emerald City umbrella maker U.N. Fold.

'Ironic,' Milo thought at the number of umbrellas in his hands. The craftsman was having a drought in business because, even though there was a rainstorm, the weather was usually so good in Oz that no one knew who he was. It had made U.N. Fold so happy to work that Milo had perhaps asked for more than he needed. Ulysses Numner had made for Milo five travel umbrellas in Winkie Yellow, Quadling Red, Munchkin Blue, Gilliken Purple, Emerald City Green, and two weekend umbrellas with one having a rainbow pattern for Saturday and a lily white pattern for Sunday. Milo wasn't unhappy about having so many umbrellas because it rained incessantly in Milo's part of Kentucky. It was never possible to have too many umbrellas in his opinion. I pay such attention to Milo's umbrellas because they'll become important later, so don't get bored reading about them. In fact don't get bored at all.

"Ribbit," E Bused murmured nearby.

The Toad Jester E. Bused was casually sitting nearby causally on a plain wooden stool under the dripping water of another leak that had sprung in the

The Wooing of Ozma

Emerald Palace's roof. E. Bused had discovered being dry was no fun at all for a toad, and thus had chosen the room with the biggest leak he could find. Rapsy the Hissing-Wing was curled up in one corner banging his head against the floor in enjoyment. Hissing wings love that, as I've said, and freedom to do this as often as he wanted was an experience Raspy was truly treasuring under his new master. Aside from the banging sound, the room was filled with the sound of Milo bemoaning his current predicament.

"Oh moan, be moan my current predicament," Milo said, looking at his toad-friend. "This situation is green indeed."

"Perhaps you should take off those emerald glasses then." E. Bused suggested as his eyes darted too and fro following a nearby fly. When he caught it, the fly shouted for help and E. Bused let it go. It wasn't very nice to devour flies who could talk back, even when one was really hungry.

"That's not what I mean. Besides, the palace would still be emerald and you'd still be green as well. I have spoken with my parents, family, and friends with Ozma's two way Magic Picture. Though initially shocked to be contacted by such means, I must say they have taken my resolution to stay in Oz very well if I promise to visit..." Milo lifted up his rainbow umbrella and shook it like a saber. "It was a hard decision, but one that must be made."

E. Bused smirked. "That reminds me of a joke. Did you hear the one about the young man who fell in love with a princess at first glance and decided to give away everything to pursue her?"

Charles Phipps

"No I can't say I have." Milo looked at E. Bused, suspecting the what the man's punch line would be. Unfortunately for Milo, it was not going to be less line and more punch.

"Well you told it to me," The Toad hopped upside down and started walking around the emerald room on his hands. "If I had a home to go back to then I certainly wouldn't be staying here."

"You have Zo." Milo pointed out to his amphibian friend.

"My point exactly," E. Bused sighed. "Hmmm I think I will ask the Princess Ozma to turn me into a giant piece of chocolate cake so that everyone will like me who looks upon me. Everyone loves chocolate." the Toad smiled broadly.

"The problem with chocolate cake, however, is that you can only love it once." Milo pointed out.

"True, perhaps I'll ask to be a very big piece then," E. Bused said smiling. "Perhaps I will ask to be turned into a full blooded Munchkin so I can be the only one in the world which doesn't breathe fire and chase little ones to terrify them."

"Methinkssssssssss your perception of the situations issssss ssssssslightly ssssskewed," Raspy murmured as he looked at E. Bused with one of his glowing red eyes. He blinked a bit until it was plain old grey. Despite how scary it looks, having glowing eyes is usually quite painful for monsters and most avoid it having them when they can. Not to mention the light from them makes it exceptionally difficult to sleep.

"Skewed? The Princess once tried to have my eyes removed for having said that she looked like she could

The Wooing of Ozma

use some more beauty rest one day, but never ever have I been skewed,"

E. Bused murmured and continued to jump around, practicing his tumbling. Frankly, E. Bused's stories of life with Princess Zoam were making even Raspy slightly uneasy.

Thankfully, such words did not have to be dealt with much longer because a group of the palace's residents took the time to visit the newcomers to their home. The Scarecrow, Professor H.M. Wogglebug T.E., Sir Hokus of Pokus, the Cowardly Lion, and the Wizard himself were all interim residents now of the Palace of Ozma because of the recent flooding. Awakened by news of an invasion, they had come to hear the news straight from the horse's mouth. Polychrome, of course, was spinning behind the group, hoping to introduce her friends to one another.

"Funny, they don't look like superstitious peasants that can't understand natural weather formations." The Scarecrow looked at the three and then at Professor Wogglebug.

"Errrr uhhh...." Professor Wogglebug winced his elongated eyes. The Wogglebug was the head of the only known university in Oz and while respected imeasurably for his great knowledge of all subjects but any put into practice, he occasionally jumped to unflattering conclusions about people. It had something to do with his head being swelled along with the rest of his body when he was turned from a tiny wogglebug into a highly magnified one with a magical lantern.

"Actually one looks like a young man, another a giant walking toad, and the other a...well errr..." the

Charles Phipps

Scarecrow racked his brains to describe Raspy. To the Scarecrow the Wogglebug's initial thoughts on the cause of the rainstorm and who the people who talked of invasion were rather off.

"I rather think it resembles a cross between a toucan, an ox, and a hommernith with a tiger's claws. I encountered the former two on my journeys across the world and the latter here in Oz," the Wizard pointed out. "And if I don't miss my guess, it is actually one of the noble race of Hissing-Wings."

"Noble race?" Raspy looked up.

"If they are any relations to dragons I must daresay that I have to slayeth you." Sir Hokus lifted up his sword proudly before the Scarecrow forced it down violently. Sir Hokus wasn't actually from Pokus but it had been where he'd been exiled when he was enchanted as an old man. Thanks to the bravery of the people of the Emerald City he'd eventually been disenchanted and become a King. Hence of course he was attending Ozma Week and quite interested in seeing if these strangers were going to be a proper addition to his lady liege.

"All this talk about slayings is very unhealthy, especially since you can't do it in Oz and I'm very glad of it! So please put your sword away before he gets the wrong idea." The Scarecrow bowed his head and casually hid the sword in his straw. "I am the Scarecrow and these are my friends…"

The Scarecrow introduced each in turn and no one interrupted, not even the Professor or Polychrome. The former is notorious for interrupting, and as you know, Polychrome had already met the trio quite early on in this chronicle. The Scarecrow was the former king of

The Wooing of Ozma

Oz once Emperor of the Silver Isles after all, and one doesn't interrupt ex-royalty twice over at work.

"A pleasure to meet you all…" Milo went up and shook the Scarecrow's hand, accidentally removing it.

"Oh blasted wet straw…" The Scarecrow murmured taking back his hand and trying desperately to put it back on right.

"AHHH!" Milo backed away in horror as E. Bused fell onto the ground laughing out loud.

"Am I really part of a noble race?" Raspy asked, rather rudely ignoring everyone else. However, it was not often that one discovers that one's race was noble wasn't a race when one had been told most of one's life it was one's job to be unpleasant.

"Oh yes, the Hissing Wings are actually quite benevolent protectors of Oz, though no one has seem them in over a generation since they all flew into the air one day and never returned," The Wizard said, remembering the incident in his past that was rather early in his rule. It was when he was still fighting off the Witches of the West and East when his old allies had disappeared.

"Oh hahahaha heehheheehe." E. Bused continued rolling on the ground. "This is funnier than you falling in love for that fairy queen." The Toad found body parts falling off very funny, though it's something of an acquired taste in humor.

"Hello all." Milo Trustworthy Starling said. He was a bit nervous around these folk. It didn't take a rocket scientist, who are not known for their romantic skill anyway, to tell that the closest friends of a queen might be more than a little protective of her if they

Charles Phipps

found a practically complete stranger falling in love with her.

"Oh which fairy queen? Maybe I know her." Polychrome danced over and looked into Milo's eyes, which made him distinctly uncomfortable.

"Well you see it's rather…" Milo was going to say complicated but again he came across his vow never to lie to Ozma. It was really very simple. He had looked upon Ozma and fallen instantly in love with the beautiful magnificent woman who was everything that the lady Zoam was not and more. It is amazing how many causal lies are routinely told in conversation nowadays, even by polite young gentlemen.

"Let's see there's Ozma…." The Scarecrow struggled his brains to remember any other fairy princesses he knew.

"Got it in one," E. Bused said to the Scarecrow.

"My brains are functioning perfectly as always." Scarecrow smiled and touched the bran brains. The Scarecrow was hoping they weren't being affected too much by the damp.

"SCOUNDREL! FIEND! I challenge you to a duel!" Sir Hokus drew his sword again before he remembered the Scarecrow had taken it and he was holding nothing but empty air.

Polychrome squealed with delight and gave the young man a hug. Although she didn't know the man very well she already counted him among her closest friends, which was a credit to them both. "But Sir Hokus, this is a good thing! I won't have you skewering my friend especially when he's fallen in love with another friend."

The Wooing of Ozma

"Skewer! Bah! It isn't a proper romance unless there is a duel! I am merely doing my part!" Sir Hokus rummaged through the Scarecrow, which sent the straw man into peels of laughter due to the tickling sensation of it all. Retrieving his sword, Sir Hokus then tipped it to his head in a salute. "Congratulations Good Sir! I expect you to prepare to face me on the fields of honor at your first opportunity."

"Oh dear, there will be all sorts of legal repercussions for this, and accounting, oh dear, and the genealogy tree will have to be updated." Professor Wogglebug, who counted himself as Oz's foremost scholar (even as others preferred to avoid counting him at all) was struck the hardest by the news.

"I still don't know what this hassssss to do with my being of a noble race." Raspy murmured.

The Wizard walked over to the Hissing-Wing and removed a tin from his pocket, offering Raspy three of the pills in it. "Here man, these will help you with that sore throat of yours. Don't be ashamed of it. All of us are feeling a bit under the weather these days." The Wizard was cycling through a number of possibilities in his head, but his look was amazingly pleased.

Milo at this point stood up and unfolded his umbrella to make a speech as the leaks had sadly spread through the room. The moment he opened the umbrella everyone but Milo hit the deck. Milo then realized that opening an umbrella indoors in a land where superstitions were mostly true was probably not a good idea. Folding back the umbrella Milo then said, "Yes indeed, I am in love with the fairy princess Lady Ozma, and by the heavens above and the master of the universe as my witness I swear…"

Charles Phipps

The Scarecrow covered Polycrome's ears. "Please, there are ladies present."

Milo ignored that, given it wasn't that type of swearing. to say "I shall woo the Lady Ozma and win her heart as she has won mine." which as a statement, it would have caused quite a few problems if the Tinman were present but thankfully he was elsewhere chopping wood for the repair of the palace in his waterproof stainless steel slicker.

"What's wooing mean?" the Cowardly Lion asked.

"It's like wow except more oooo less ow." Polychrome explained as she took the Scarecrow's wet gloves off her ears.

"Ooo, you should read to her from the Princables Mathmatica! That is the most romantic book of poetry in Oz!" Professor Wogglebug exclaimed happily.

"You should do what I did to win my two wives. Offer her a cave and plenty of food for the rest of her life." the Cowardly Lion proclaimed.

"I didn't know you were married Lion!" Scarecrow looked overjoyed "When do I get to meet the Missuses?"

"Hopefully you never will. There is a reason I was living in the Emerald City, even before the rainstorm," The Cowardly Lion said dryly.

"There is only one sure fire way to win a maiden's heart, and that is to rescue her from a Dragon," Sir Hokus said. "My old friend George did it all the time and he was never one to be unpopular with the ladies of the court, and neither was Lance."

Milo looked curiously at Sir Hokus after that peculiar and quite telling statement. "Well, as much as I appreciate the advice, sir, I must point out the rather

The Wooing of Ozma

obvious fact that the Lady Ozma is in no danger of being taken by dragons, nor would I wish it on her even if she was." Milo waved his umbrella about like a sword but being a pacifist, would never pick up a true weapon.

"Oh. Well then never mind. The theory is still sound however." Sir Hokus huffed and puffed.

The Wizard smiled as he put his arm around Milo's neck and tugged him real close. "My boy, you have come to the right place for advice. I have to tell you that I, Oscar Zoroaster Phadrig Issac Norman Henkle Emmanuel Ambroise Diggs, just call me Oz, am the greatest expert on romance that you will ever find in this kingdom. I have studied at the feet of great poets in India and made the ladies of Paris swoon with my style. Cassanova himself was put to shame."

"Cassanova died in the 15th century I believe." Milo pointed out.

"Details my boy, Details." The Wizard began leading Milo from the room as the others continued to give their advice.

Polychrome watched as she began a few spins through the water puddles that formed in the palace chambers and then said to herself, "I have a bad feeling Milo is going to get himself into a bit of trouble with that advice." And as usual, the warnings of fairies are a bit too accurate for comfort.

Chapter Seven

The rainstorm outside the Emerald Palace of Ozma continued its terrible downpour on Oz. Still, it had lightened up considerably in strength because Igor was taking a break from pedaling for sleep and then breakfast. It was in this climate that the Wizard of Oz and Milo Starling were preparing for the first stage of their plan for Milo to woo Ozma. Unfortunately, like all great plans, there was a bit of discussion as to what exactly should be the execution of it…

"I understand you are trying to be helpful Mister Oz. However I…" Milo didn't quite know how to express how silly he felt. Truth be told the young mortal had some reason to be questioning of the Wizard's choice in attire; he was dressed in a five colored tunic with leggings, pointed shoes, a elaborate green hat that was nearly his size. The obscenely large headgear draped over the top of his head and backside and hurt to wear. The strange costume was completed by the mandolin hanging around his neck.

"My boy I can assure you that this dress will melt the Lady Ozma's heart like nothing that she has ever seen before. It shall be merely the coupe de gras to winning her favor when you serenade her with the fine playing of the instrument of troubadours," the Wizard strummed the device gently before beckoning to Ozma's window up above them.

"Yes about that Sir. I hate to be a spoiler but…I don't know how to play the mandolin. Actually to be honest my father never taught or had it arranged for me to learn how to sing, dance, or do any of such things," Milo Starling strummed the instrument for a moment

The Wooing of Ozma

and it made a sound eerily similar to a cat being strangled.

"Eeeeeh. Best not to let Eureka hear that noise, my boy. What sort of man keeps his son from learning how to play an instrument though…." The Wizard frowned slightly as he twirled the umbrella he had borrowed from Milo. "It's truly a valuable life skill and one only a gross villain would deprive his son of such."

"My father was an insurance salesman Sir Wizard," Milo said frowning at the insult to his family.

"Say no more my boy. That explains everything," The Wizard shook his head at the terrible memory of the relentless enemies of man he had known back in the United States. "They are the only people I know who can persuade a man to pay money for hoping that your home will not burn down."

Milo thought it better than to defend the trade that, while admittedly queer, had provided a roof over his head and put him to school. Any argument would also be tainted by the fact he looked silly. "Yes. So perhaps can we avoid the mandolin playing and singing?"

The Wizard shook his head sternly and lifted up a hand to the rapidly getting wet Milo. It was part of the Wizard's plan that the young man look exceedingly pathetic in order to win sympathy from the Queen. The Wizard hadn't let the young man in on that part of the plan however. "Never! It doesn't matter how badly you play young man the woman will eat it up," the Wizard assured him.

Ever since he had accepted the existence of magical flying kingdoms, toads that could talk, and the existence of the angel upon the Earth Ozma, Milo was less reticent than he might be about strange actions. Even if it was unpleasant and foolish he was glad to try just about anything in hopes of pleasing the lady.

"As you wish," Milo cleared his throat "Thank you Sir, I shall begin the wooing process immediately." Milo knew personally very few love songs and none of them he knew the music to so he decided to sing from his heart.

As the Wizard heard his well intentioned but rather off key efforts he looked into his pocket where some of his baby pigs rested. "Perhaps you were right and I should have made time for giving the boy some of Professor Wogglebug's singing pills."

The pigs looked up at the noise coming into their warm resting place and nodded with disapproving snouts.

Milo's singing however bad it should be noted came from a loving heart.

Despite all of its off key nature and occasionally irritable tone it was a good song. It spoke of Ozma's beauty, the justice of her to her subjects, and what feelings he felt whenever he looked upon her. It also sang of the feelings he thought she might have of being alone in her tower. It was a very large assumption but one dead on the mark. However because Kentucky boys are known for their heart but not their poetry it will be best if we wait a few years to string them together into something that actually does resemble a song. Then when we print what exactly he did sing, it won't embarrass the poor man.

You'll forgive us.

***

The Wooing of Ozma

Ozma listened to the strange noises outside of her bedroom and looked out of her tower upon Milo. The young man was making quite a few strange noises from his mandolin. Though no sun shown out in the sky because of the terrible rainstorm, which drowned out all the true light in Oz, the true ruler of Oz knew it was almost time for sunrise. The words were especially appropriate though, even if Ozma wasn't sure what to make of them all. Ozma had been unable to sleep this night for fear of something dreadful and also a wistful longing. She had even retrieved the Magic Belt to protect her from harm but while the relic stolen from the Nome King calmed her fears about being kidnapped or attacked, it did nothing to quel the ache in her heart.

"Is someone strangling Eureka?" the Sawhorse asked walking into the room from Ozma's workshop, or as he called it 'his bedroom'.

"No," Ozma said looking down and hardly spared her old friend a glance.

"Pity," The Sawhorse said with perhaps less than complete tact.

Ozma looked back at the Sawhorse with a slightly amused but mostly disapproving look. "Actually no, it's the newest member of our court playing the mandolin and singing to me in an attempt to woo me." Ozma couldn't help but admit how ill-advised the scheme was, it was very flattering.

"Didn't you place a ban on people singing outside your window Ozma?" The Sawhorse asked.

Ozma remembered the rather unpleasant series of incidents, which had become rather intolerable a few decades back. It had started rather early with Winkies, Munchkins, Gillikens, Quadlings, and stranger folk from Oz coming regularly to the court of the Emerald City to pay court to her. Some were doing it because they honestly believed they were in love with the Princess.

While others were actually, to her gall, simply trying to become royalty or gain wealth by seducing her. The constant stream of would-be-lovers had resulted in her placing a ban on anyone singing outside her window. It was necessary so that the Princess could get some sleep. Ozma would have placed a ban on the sending of love poetry and chocolate but frankly she rather enjoyed both on rainy mornings like this.

"We had better get him to stop...for our ears and his freedom," the Sawhorse said putting his two wooden legs against the side of his head.

Ozma looked down at Milo before going over to the side of her bed.

"Perhaps...this one is different somehow," Ozma immediately regretted the words but didn't retract them. The ruler of Oz didn't really know that this one was any different than the others and she had only known him a few minutes. Dorothy's descriptions of the nice young gentleman however and she had rather glowingly described his heroism against the Hissing-Wings. Ozma wasn't entirely taken in though by her closest friends account that the man was good. How truly could a man fall in love with a woman after only a few moments in her presence? It was ridiculous not only in concept but in reality! Did these men not have sweethearts or others that they might fall love or be loved by back home? Did these men not know that her

The Wooing of Ozma

kingdom and subjects would always come first above them? Did they not know mortal's marriages to faeries always ended in heartache? Did she? The last question struck home in her heart.

"Princess it looks like your face could use some sanding. The weather seems to have worn it down," The Sawhorse looked up at Ozma and placed its head on her legs. Ozma patted her creation on the head and smiled at him dimly.

"It's not the weather Sawhorse...as miserable as it is," Ozma looked outside at the drizzle of cold sleet that hadn't stopped since the afternoon. "I suppose we should invite Milo in from the rain. It's a terrible storm outside and I wouldn't want him to catch his pain from cold," Death from cold of course did not exist in Oz.

Ozma got up from the side of her bed and headed for the door before the Sawhorse said something, which stopped her. "Princess Ozma if you dislike having so many suitors why not simply pick one and be done with it? Perhaps the others will stop offering themselves if they know you already have one."

Ozma thought about that decision quite frankly. "I guess none of them ever appealed to me that way," it was a simple answer but simple answers were usually the right ones in Ozma's opinion. Certainly quite a few of her suitors were likable in their own way but would Ozma really want to share every intimate moment of her life with them? Would Ozma be willing to share the troubles of the kingdom or dare she say it...times when she was not so regal? None of them could balance the love she wanted and appreciation for the duty to her kingdom in her mind. They wanted either a queen they could serve or a loving wife but neither one was Ozma for she would both.

"I'll never understand meat people," The Sawhorse said simply. "It's a very good thing I'll never have to find a mate. One Sawhorse is definitely enough in the land of Oz."

Princess Ozma smiled as she descended the steps of her palace she felt a slight chill to her body. Ozma looked around the various dripping droplets of water with concern. The fact her palace was flooding seemed like a terrible omen of things to come. In Oz everything was tied to a ruler and if a ruler's home was breaking thus was the sign that something was wrong with the ruler herself or was soon to be. The bottom of the stairs leading to the outside Palace Grounds was actually slightly flooded and Ozma had to lift up her nightgown to avoid getting it wet. Her bare feet were rather cold from the water that nearly reached her ankles.

"Princess Ozma I presume?" a voice spoke from behind her. The voice was melodic in its own way and belonged to a fairy Ozma was sure of it. The accent was Ozzian though it was a bit deeper than Ozma's own and had a sort of understated malice. Which made Ozma wonder who it could be. When Ozma turned around, she came face to face with her mirror image. The woman had her eyes, body, and even flowers in her ears (though they were ugly lilies instead of poppies and made her look like she was attending a funeral instead of living her life to the fullest). Ozma had never once attended a funeral but had heard them described long enough to know that they were places she'd rather not visit. The woman was also wearing a

The Wooing of Ozma

raven feather dress that made her blend in well with the darkness around. Ozma felt for her wand at her side before she realized that she'd left it on the table next to her bed.

"Yes and you are Princess Zoam," Ozma said. Ozma had no doubt this was the ruler of the strange country of Zo that had been described to her.

"I must admit you are much prettier than I thought you'd be." The ruler of Zo smiled at Ozma with her red stained lips.

Ozma backed away slightly, the Princess looked up to the Sawhorse to see if he perhaps he might be able to offer some assistance. Ozma saw her friend and mount then run into a tall man dressed in a military uniform. He was not ugly but had the same cruel expression to his face Zoam had.

"Hello sir. You must be one of the famous Ozian wonders that we've heard so much about," Igor Lackey said to the Sawhorse which merely stood proud before the unpleasant human. The Sawhorse had seen plenty of evil wizards in his time and this one was no different.

"Thank you very much. As I understand it we're related. The blood of the fairy has always carried stronger on the female line than the male. I must request however you stop making rain over my country because it is flooding it and destroying many of my subject's homes." Princess Ozma decided now was a good a time as any to bring up.

"Are you a good ruler or a bad ruler?" Princess Zoam rather rudely ignoring her question.

"I beg your pardon?" Ozma asked. It was very strange but staring at her twin she felt something other than pity for the woman whom might have been her twin. It was fear, she was sure of it.

"Are you a good ruler or a bad ruler? Do you care about your subjects or are they just there for your amusement? I find that once I stopped caring about my subjects that I started to enjoy my job a great deal more," Princess Zoam said as she walked closer.

"I most certainly do care about my subjects," Ozma said at Princess Zoam. "Perhaps you should consider stopping being a ruler and finding some other profession." the words that came out of her mouth were curiously less forceful than she usually was when upset. The experience of being afraid was something that Ozma remembered well enough from her time as Tip but since Ozma had been restored she'd rarely felt the emotion. Ozma felt fear now. That family could look upon her with such utter contempt. That her own face could hide such a villain, was terrible!

Princess Zoam's face then softened a considerable bit as she smiled "Actually I do intend to change my professions quite soon." the words were soothing and Ozma was momentarily taken in by the act of the Princess. Stranger things had happened in Oz than such random acts of repentance.

"Yes I think I'll change my job from ruling Zo to ruling Oz." Princess Zoam lifted up her wand at her. As the Sawhorse tried to bolt past Igor the evil sorceress turned her wand on the wooden marvel and transformed it into a small toy figurine.

"No!" Ozma then launched herself at the evil Princess, just before a series of ropes burst from Zoam's wands and tied her up like a cattle in a lasso. Ozma was bound and gagged with another wave of the

The Wooing of Ozma

evil princess's wand. The Palace should be rising soon however but if they could not hear Ozma's cry what good would it do?

Igor walked down the stairs of the Emerald Palace hall where he looked at Zoam and said. "Take her wishing belt,"

Ozma blinked and winced in extreme agony but before she could wiggle her toe and make a wish the Nome King's powerful magical item was stripped away from her. She had been thinking so much about Milo and her relative's evil that she had forgotten about the most important thing she had! Ozma could only watch in horror as Princess Zoam put the object around her own waist.

"I wish I was ruler of the world," Princess Zoam said with extreme glee as she performed the actions perfectly to activate it. It had been easy to learn the instructions from the citizens of Oz because the tales of Dorothy and Ozma's travels had become so commonplace. The belt shuddered and glowed for a brief moment but as much as Zoam would like the world to be covered in statues of her and all the history books saying the countries of the World were called Zoamland, Zoam Country, the Zoamnited States of Zoamerica, or whatnot the wishing belt merely made a fizzling sound and slightly smoked.

Ozma only groaned and rolled her eyes with the gag in her mouth. Thinking to herself what a close call that was that they had not made a lesser wish. The Nome King's belt was powerful indeed but it was most powerful only in fairy country and trying to extend it all over the world merely caused it to fail. It would take at least a day for the magic in the belt to replenish itself and that would give her friends time to uncover Zoam's evil.

"Perhaps we should work with smaller wishes first Your Wrathful Divineness. It is almost time for the residents of this palace to awaken and we need to spirit away our prisoner here before they take note of her abcense. You have to be here of course to allay such fears," Igor said pointing a long finger at Zoam's chest.

"Yes. A great pity that she has such…dull clothing I will have to dress myself in," Princess Zoam said even as Ozma frowned intensely, she was quite fond of her wardrobe though of course she was much more worried about her kingdom right now. "Place her in cold iron bars Igor. If your minions do half the job that you say they will, then the Great book of Records will be ours and no one will ever suspect dear Princess Ozma is going to spend the rest of her life in a tower in Zo."

The two of them shared an evil grin that made Ozma feel sick to her stomach. Cold iron was the bane of all faeries and even if she got her hands and mouth free there was no vocal spell of hers that could penetrate their numbing power. Ozma's last sight before a group of poppies were placed in front of her face and their smell put her into a deep sleep was that of the Glass Cat. The small creation of Doctor Pipt's was spying upon the entire affair from the top of the stairs!

"If ever your heart was not cold…" Ozma pleaded through the gag in her mouth. The Princess hoped that Bungle could carry on news of her kidnapping to the others in the Palace but such thoughts soon left her.

The Wooing of Ozma

The dreamless slumber of the magical flowers had overtaken her.

***

Milo finished his heartfelt song and sat down on a nearby emerald bench in the courtyard where he was singing. The poppies inside the garden were the most abundant flower present, but they were hardly the only one. In a way they were the least strange of them all and thus all the more wondrous to Milo. The minister to be longed for some of his home but he knew that his place was here now somehow. It was cosmic. It would take some getting used to though. There were trees which grew lunch pails, another which grew chocolate, another lollipops, and in general an orchard of confections that made Milo wonder just how everyone managed to stay so thin and beautiful around here.

"I-regret-to-inform-you-that-you-are-under-arrest," A strong metal clanging voice spoke to him before he felt a very cold bronze hand on his shoulder.

Turning to his side Milo found himself face to face with a very large man that somewhat resembled a cross between a robot and a tea kettle. It took him a few moments to realize that this must be the figure Polychrome mentioned as Tik-tok. Milo was a bit absent minded by nature and stopped for a second to realize what exactly the man had just said. "Pardon me Sir but did you just inform me that I was under arrest?"

The Metal man then said "Yes-I-did. You-have-vio-lated-the-Prin-cess-Ozma's-decree-against-woo-ing."

Milo looked at his mandolin and pulled off his completely ridiculous looking hat. "Am I to understand

Charles Phipps

that such an activity is frowned upon in the Land of Oz?" Admittedly, if Milo were the ruler he too would have considered banning wooing that involved such outlandish gear as he was wearing. However the process in general was quite time honored and if someone wished to wear the idiotic attire he couldn't in all honesty object.

"Only-when-it-is-the-woo-ing-of-the-Princess-herself," Tik-Tok said simply.

Milo stopped for a moment as he got up. "Even if the man in question is in love with her?" Milo felt absolutely silly falling in love at first sight but he couldn't deny what he felt. He was a man who trusted first impressions and there was not anything about Ozma that did not speak of one experience that Milo wanted to know more about. It had been her eyes which had done it. While Zoam's had been vacant and cold there was an immense sense of duty and compassion for all in the world in Ozma's. Milo had always wanted to meet a person that way because it was the same desire which drove him every second of the day.

"As-a-mach-ine-I-can-neither-feel-love-nor-hate-so-I-do-not-know-why-men-put-them-selves-through-so-much-to-win-her-hand-but-I-do-know-that-all-whom-I-have-dragged-out-of-here-before-also-insisted-that-they-loved-her." TikTok's rhythmic voice was slightly unsettling to Milo.

"Anyone willing to be corrected is on the pathway to life. Anyone refusing has lost his chance," Milo quoted one of his favorite proverbs.

"That-is-sound-advice." Tik Tok said taking Milo by the hand as he led him out of the courtyard.

The Wooing of Ozma

"I'm afraid not for me it isn't Goodsir constable. The Good Book is a tome filled with wonderful reference and beautiful knowledge but I will not apply its advice here. For you see, I do not believe what I do is a mistake. No matter what the penalty is, I shall continue to woo the Lady Ozma and try to make her love me in return," Milo Starling said resolved.

"Even-if-the-penalty-is-death?" Tik Tok asked.

"The penalty is death?" Milo asked shocked. He had seen many things in Oz but had never heard anything so horrible for such. Still he was of a trusting nature enough to assume that there was a good reason for such or more likely something was up with his bronze friend here.

"No. How-ever-most-whom-I-ask-the-question-cease-their-attempts-at-woo-ing-before-asking-such." Tik Tok merrily walked along towards the Emerald Palace's dungeon which as you know who have read the previous chronicles is a four poster bedroom with a small library and pleasant view of the city.

Milo was considerably relieved as you might guess he would be "Well every man has a full measure of life. The question is what he does with it. Better to fall and die for something worth dying for than living for not the highest of graces." Milo was, as we said, a bit of a poetic youth at sixteen. While most of his quotes were from the Good Book and Ben Franklin he did have a slight flare with words.

"This-is-Oz. No-one-can-die. So-your-best-advice-is-to-live-for-the-thing-worth-dying-for," Tik Tok said simply as he locked Milo inside the room. Ironically the Dungeon was now the only room in the Emerald

Palace that wasn't leaking water into it. So it was a benefit in disguise.

"Advice I hope to follow noble Tik Tok. Good day to you." Milo removed his emerald glasses and cleaned them while he spoke through the door. Just because a man was arresting him didn't mean there was any reason to be impolite to him. He'd been much the same to the Slavercruds who had kidnapped him off the ground on the way to church, once the initial screaming had stopped.

"Good-day-to-you-as-well-Sir," Tik-Tok said.

As the thunder clapped Milo got a distinct unpleasant feeling however that something was going terribly wrong in Oz. Milo had the fullest confidence that Princess Ozma would, with her friends defeat the evils of Zo, but he couldn't escape the idea that this was his fault. As far as Milo knew the Island of Zo was above in the sky simply because the Princess wanted him. The hero of this story didn't want to cause trouble to such nice people but nor did he want to go back to Zo.

'The wicked man's fears will all come true and so will the good man's hopes.' Milo reassured himself but if it came down to a choice between returning to Zo or becoming a serpent to this paradise he would summon what courage he could and leave before further harm came to Oz because of him. Milo having not slept this night prepared for bed and said his evening prayers (despite it being morning), mentioning specifically the Land of Oz in them. If he knew what troubles were brewing Milo might have included the entire world.

The Wooing of Ozma
Chapter Eight

Glinda sat upon her ruby throne and listened to the complaints of all the Quadlings who came to tell of the rain's effect on the South of Oz. Glinda had spent most of the night working away at her cauldron, trying to come up with a spell which would remove the rainstorm that the wizards in Zo had cooked up. Unfortunately, despite all of her magic, she could do nothing to make any effect whatsoever on the rainstorm of Zo.

"It's absolutely terrible Miss Glinda. My walking Potato crop can't stand this much rain! Unless they get into shelter…and I can't lift all those potatoes up into my walking house before they're soggy and once walking potatoes get soggy they can't walk anywhere!" Farmer Benson Brown sobbed. He was a Quadling of considerable skill in breeding strange and wonderful crops but he had paid for this skill with a remarkable lack of common sense.

Glinda lifted up her right hand and said "Farmer Brown have you considered simply asking your potato crop to move to the place where you want it to go?"

"Your wisdom shall be spoken of by all Quadlings for ages to come!" Farmer Brown bowed his head on the ground and then exited before Glinda blinked and shook her head.

"I hope not," The Good Witch murmured. It was much the same with the rest of the Quadling people. The China Country were in particularly bad shape because the land the dish-wear inhabited was a valley that had been transformed into a Lake. The best Glinda could for the people had been to send them a magical box of ever-full soap detergent. After all it was always good to make the best of a bad situation. As it neared daybreak Glinda arose from her throne and contented herself that the last of the Quadlings had been dealt with to the best of her abilities. Still, she knew that the situation was going to get rapidly worse.

"Do you think Lady Glinda that there is anything the Princess can do?" Mary Anne the second in command of the Good Witch of the South's defenses asked.

It was a largely ceremonial duty that had no real purpose usually other than to keep general order in supplicants and also handle her day-to-day affairs such as cleaning up and dinner preparation. Men she discovered were remarkably less suited for such and far less sweet appearing doing so.

"Perhaps. The Wishing Belt could probably transfer the kingdom of Zo to an entirely different realm or into a peaceful white cloud but we need to know why they are placing this storm over our civilization. Despite Oz's suffering we do not know enough about its cause to act rashly…" Glinda was personally actually fairly sure something dramatic did need to be done, however. She would be heading to the Emerald City as soon as she had finished her rest. She was at present, in no shape to think on the problem.

"SQUAAAAAWWWWWWWWWK" a terrifying yowl ran through the halls and Glinda knew exactly where it came from. Glinda's reading room of which held the Book of Records.

It was very difficult to run in her gown but Glinda made the best of it and emerged into the reading room

The Wooing of Ozma

where she was immediately overpowered by the smell that was present. Slavercruds, who were among the most loathsome of faeries. The obese bearded creatures gave off an odor that was their primary weapon but were very strong and could fly. It was mainly because of their odor that they served the Unseelie Court because they felt (wrongly) few others would tolerate them if they were good.

"SQUAAAWWWKK There is the Witch! Take the book to the Princess while we deal with her," the leader of the ten or twelve cattle sized monsters said to his soldierly as one of them turned and absconded with Glinda's magical tome.

The leader then waved for the rest of the his small army to charge at the Good Witch of the South with weapons, claws, and gnashing large ugly teeth.

Glinda thought it must be usually quite terrifying and horrible to the people that they encountered normally.

"I want you all to become docile little sheep. Pyrzqxglyl!" Glinda said causally waving her wand a variant on the very powerful transforming spell Pyrzqxgl. The spell turned every one of the Slavercruds who had stayed to attack the Good Witch of the South into harmless lambs. The Slavercruds transformed bah'ed happily at their new form save for the men who enjoyed ramming each others heads into one another but otherwise Glinda was just glad to get the terrible smell out of her chambers.

"Lady Glinda I'm readying the Guard…oh." Mary Anne came bursting into the room and seemed rather disappointed at the Good Witch of the South's easy handling of the most rude intruders.

Charles Phipps

"There, there Mary Anne." Glinda pinched her guardswoman on the cheek. "Go back to your sewing. Please also inform my swans that they shall have to wear specially crafted umbrellas over themselves because we are going to the Emerald City this morning."

The rainstorm while horrific was an act that could be dealt with causally but the stealing of her Book of Records was something else entirely. It spoke of a much more malign intelligence at foot here. Like Ugu the Shoemaker the current attacker knew something of Oz's magical treasures and if they did then they would no doubt make a play for the Wishing Belt as well. They must have had some sort of scrying ability to detect Oz's treasures since like the Wishing Belt, the Book of Records which recorded everything that happened in Oz was brought into Glinda's posession well after the Zoites had been exiled.

Mary Anne frowned and nodded. "I'm making a very nice sweater for my niece Lady Glinda." the guardswoman walked off, rather disappointed, to perform her orders. Glinda always loved taking in such expressive youth because it was good for all of Oz if such desires for adventures were quenched early. Adventure was wonderful but occurred quite often naturally without the need to seek it.

Glinda then turned down to the lambs on the ground of her palace. "I now must deal with you my small woolen friends." her eyebrows crossed and she let the furry creatures let them know in no uncertain terms that she was not happy with them.

"Miss Glinda would you…bahhhhh…be willing to transform us back into our natural forms if we tell you

The Wooing of Ozma

everything we know about Zo and Zoam?" the leader of the Slavercruds who had also been turned into sheep asked.

"I'm afraid not. By stealing the Book of Records you've proven yourself quite capable of hurting other people. So, I will likely not turn you back. However if you are good then I will allow you to graze peacefully on the back of my estate provided you do not harm any of my flowers." Glinda made what was she thought a fairly generous offer despite her anger.

The leader of the Slavercruds bowed his head and bahed. "Verrry well Lady Glinda. I was just testing you anyway. Being a sheep is much more preferrable to being a smelly Slavercrud. We won't be baahd anymore. We'll beeeee glaaaahd to tell you everything we know about the people of Zo and why we were here. However can we have some graaaaaass while we do it?"

Glinda nodded to her new informant and learned much.

***

Ozma swung gently in her cage like a bird as she looked out the large amount of Ozites that had been imprisoned within the walls of this terrible prison.

They filled the Dungeons of Zo completely it seemed. It broke her heart to see any creature held prisoner, but the sheer massive number of them behind bars in this place was an abomination the likes she had never seen before. The cold iron made her extremely uncomfortable and all Ozma could give them were re-assuring words to the few subjects that could hear her.

Charles Phipps

"I want you to make sure that the Princess under NO circumstances ever leaves this dungeon. Don't harm her though. The effects of bringing ill to the rightful ruler of the land might be disastrous in the extreme because Zo was once part of Oz." Igor Lackey was speaking to several large men and a very small pudgy one dressed in black suits. They were wearing the oddest glasses which were fogged with black smoke. Curiously enough they had around their necks black earmuffs despite it being mid summer. Princess Ozma wondered privately how Igor couldn't consider knocking her out with magic flowers and putting her in a cold iron cage wasn't bringing ill to her but she didn't want to give the wicked man any more reason to do her harm.

Igor turned up and looked at Princess Ozma as he pulled out a pair of black goggles from his pocket. "You should be honored Princess Ozma to be looked after by the finest soldiers in all of Zo. The Black Spectacled Guard are the only people in the land who will be unaffected by your beauty and pleasant nature no matter how sweet and innocent you appear. Put on your earmuffs gentlemen," Igor said as the Order complied.

"And why is that?" Ozma said, not feeling very honored at all.

"The Black Spectacled Order wear magical glasses crafted by my father Evile that cause everything they see to be reversed. Beautiful becomes ugly to them, good things they spy become evil, ugly becomes beautiful, and horrid actions become nice. They earmuffs ensure that only the most rude and belligerent can be stood in their presence for long." Igor sneered.

The Wooing of Ozma

Ozma found such a thing quite awful and seeing their looks at her realized that she must be quite horrid to them. Ozma also wondered why exactly someone would make such a stupidly mean device "You have done them a great disservice Igor Lackey by forcing them to wear such vile magical devices."

"On the contrary Princess Ozma the Black Spectacled Order are married to the meanest and ugliest women in all of Zo and see the vile citizenry we rule over as cheerful, pleasant, and serene. Their children merely have to overcome their ability to do well to be great in their parent's eyes. It is all a matter of perspective." Igor handed her a set of the goggles and smiled broadly at Ozma. Ozma could see what the man was talking about because she looked at his smile through them and only saw only a wicked scowl.

Ozma shook her head. "You merely disguise the problems of Zo Igor and eventually the goggles will bring about a greater heartache than you can imagine. No good can come of untruths."

"I have lived my entire life on untruths Princess Ozma and thus far it has brought me a great deal of what you might consider good. The Princess demands that you be kept here and for that you shall be here forever." Igor looked immensely pleased with himself and it did not take Ozma much time to deduce the situation.

"You must care for her very much. Why don't you tell her." Ozma thought she'd appeal to the man's decent side, if he had one.

Igor frowned and while the Black Spectacled Order saw it as an absolutely wonderful smile to the hideous grotesque, quite not happy to look upon, hag it was

Charles Phipps

really ferocious. "You understand very little about love Princess. There are few ways of showing one's devotion better than doing absolutely everything in your power for them but receiving absolutely nothing in return."

Ozma blinked at Igor "That sounds personally very silly to me."

"Here, Here Weather Master! It's quite right your saying doing nothing for someone and getting much for it!" the leader of the Black Spectacled Order said trying to help the dark wizard but doing of course the opposite since with his magical earmuffs he can hear nothing properly. Now there is nothing quite so disheartening to an evil man than being called on his foolishness so Igor took this moment to walk off and leave Princess Ozma alone in the dungeon.

Ozma realized that she'd have to get herself out of this mess somehow but she wasn't exactly sure how to accomplish such a goal. She had been kidnapped before and she supposed she should be grateful that this time she hadn't been turned into a peach pit but the least she could do was make the effort to escape on her own. Still escaping from the Dungeons of Zo was not going to be easy. The bars were too close together to squeeze through, Ozma being a sensible girl who was not often in a cell up had never learned to pick locks, and her magic wouldn't work on the bars, so it was a terrible conundrum.

"Ahem! Pardon me are you Princess Ozma?" a voice spoke to the Princess before Ozma turned around and saw a very large set of chains floating around in the middle of the air.

"Yes I am." Ozma looked at the sight oddly.

The Wooing of Ozma

"Oh that's wonderful news. I'm the Snark Snark Your Princessness and I've always wanted to meet you. I heard only yesterday though that you were looking for me and had sent the wonderful Princess Dorothy to find me. If this is about breaking Mayor Bumhug's fence then I do apologize for that was an accident." The mysterious voice continued in its words with genuine concern coming forth.

Ozma smiled at the Snark Snark's invisible form and said. "There are no hard feelings noble Snark Snark and our situation is a bit graver than your breaking down a fence I think. Though I must tell you that you will eventually have to help the Mayor repair it."

The Snark Snark snorted happily and Ozma figured that the invisible creature must have a very large trunk. "I'm glad to hear that Your Highness because I'd hate to have offended someone with my actions. If I was able to fit through the door I'd be able to fly us away on my great wings but they shrunk me down to put me in the dungeon with magic before making me big again."

Ozma did not know truly if the Snark Snark had great wings by her standards because the word 'great' was entirely up to to who was saying it. However whether he did or not a bit of a plan was forming within Ozma's head that might be able to free her and all of her people here inside.

***

Zoam walked through the halls of the Emerald Palace with a devilish glint to her eyes. While her looks were close enough to the Princess Ozma's that she was sure that no one would recognize her normally she had cast a few extra glamours on herself so that her voice, posture, and even disposition matched her cousins more closely. Zoam was sure she was going to enjoy her stay here. The Emerald Palace was much more beautiful than her obsidian one. Furthermore the dripping water and moans of the people having a bad day were all the sweeter because of the newness of them all.

"Princess Ozma?" Dorothy asked walking through the halls of the palace behind Ozma.

Zoam tried to remember who exactly this was from the commoner's descriptions of the palace's residents though it was hard to deduce because her cousin was friends with so many plain young women.

"Trot?" Princess Zoam said making a guess.

"Dorothy," Dorothy Gale said rather surprised by her best friend in the world not recognizing her voice. Of course it wasn't her but she didn't know that and we do if you know what I mean.

"Oh yes Dorothy my best friend in the world who slew the two wicked witches!" Princess Zoam smiled trying to cover her little mistake.

Personally Zoam was very afraid to be around such a horrid little girl who would kill such nice evil old women just a few days into her visit to fairy country, but she tried not to show it.

"Princess Ozma are you feeling all right?" Dorothy asked looking somewhat concerned. "Toto came down with a cold and he's still at the Doctors. I'd hate for you to come down with something in the middle of these troubles."

The Wooing of Ozma

"Ah yes Toto. Your little dog." Zoam smiled gently backing away from Dorothy.

"I truly hope he feels much better and soon but I wouldn't worry because if Oz is anything like Z…I mean no one can die in our country after all. Excuse me." Princess Zoam then ran as fast as she could down the nearest steps not stopping to see the look that Dorothy was giving her. The Princess wasn't looking much into where she was going, so she ended up slamming headfirst into the Scarecrow. The former King of the Emerald City was changing the water buckets still filling up at the stair's foot. The pair then promptly fell over all the buckets and landed in a pile a few feet away covered in water and the Scarecrow's stuffings.

"Oomph. Why don't you watch where you are going?" Princess Zoam said shouting as she spat out straw.

The Scarecrow was a terrifying thing to Princess Zoam, in Zo the only things that were animated by magic were terrible and unfriendly things usually in her service. "Oh but Princess Ozma I was looking where I was going. I was going to take the pales of water outside and dump them in the lake then I was looking at the floor and where I was tumbling."

"Oh why don't you go jump in a lake!" Princess Zoam shouted at the top of her lungs to the field born man and proceeded to stomp onto her throne room.

The Scarecrow put his right hand to his face for a moment as he thought about that. Now he was already wet enough as it is and no one likes wet straw yet Princess Ozma had never made a bad decision the

Charles Phipps

Scarecrow could recall. Also he was one of her closest friends.

"Very well if she wants me to go jump in a Lake then I suppose it is for a very good reason." the Scarecrow then propped himself up and headed towards Lake Quad.

Princess Zoam finally arrived in her throne room a few moments later severely disturbed by the two encounters, which had gone by. The throne room was full of young citizens of Oz coming in from all over the land to pay her homage and get help with their troubles. To Princess the sight of so many sad pathetic wretches coming to her for help was a warming sight to the Princess's cold heart. It would ever so much fun to her to disappoint them all.

At the front of the room Princess Ozma's maid Jellia was cleaning up the buckets of water which now numbered in the dozens through the room.

"Hello…Princess…Uhhhgh…Ozma," Jellia said lifting a bucket of water on her neck, a bucket from her teeth, a bucket in both hands, and trying to balance another on her left foot. Princess Zoam found it quite comical to look upon. The supplicants were standing rather rudely still, despite their desire to help the chamberlain maid of Oz with her bucket carrying. For many this was their view of Princess Ozma and they wanted to make a good impression. Ironic, whoever would've help her maid would have made the best one on the Princess but that's a lesson in manners for another time.

"Hello Jellia." Princess Zoam smiled. "Jellia I'd like you in addition to cleaning up this mess to do me a

The Wooing of Ozma

few small errands." the ruler of Zo gestured to the buckets "Once you get this pigsty cleaned up."

Jellia balancing the bucket on her neck with her teeth around another pail's handle answered "Er Huh? Whad's dat?"

"Well I'd like you to have all three thousand of those dresses I found in my closet burned. I've come to dislike them in their shades of my five least favorite colors red, blue, purple, green, and yellow. I'd like you to have the royal tailors craft everything in shades of white, black, and very black from this day on." Princess Zoam liked these because in Zo everything was white, black, or very black and they were her favorite colors.

"Realwy? Is dat zo?" Jellia asked continuing trying to keep her balance.

"Yes I'd also like my throne elevated three feet because frankly it just isn't high enough. You'll need to have the royal carpenters and jewelers here for that and I want it done today." Princess Zoam looked down at her feet and tapped the floor. "Hmmm tell them also I'd like a gigantic spring loaded trap door on the ground so I can toss people out the window who annoy me with their prattle."

Jellia looked at Princess Zoam oddly. "Rewy Princess Ozma dat's...strang."

"I'm not the Princess you knew." Zoam added candidly before looking Jellia over. "...And burning coals girl! You really should change your clothes! You look like a common maid."

Jellia then dropped the bucket from her mouth as she set down the other three buckets and took the

Charles Phipps

bucket off her neck into her hands. "A common maid Your Majesty?"

"Yes and frankly even a common maid wouldn't wear those shoes." Zoam commented. If Zoam were a witch these would have been her last words because Jellia took that moment to douse the false monarch with a bucket of the very rainwater she had been pouring onto Oz. Thankfully for Zoam (and Jellia who would have felt awfully guilty if she had liquidated someone) the evil Princess of Zo was merely a fairy girl and thus just drenched by the experience.

"I'll come back and return to change the water when you're in a better mood." Jellia walked out the door and slammed it behind her. Princess Zoam too stunned from her sudden wetness to consider turning the chamberlain of Ozma into snow or a tadpole or something she normally would have turned the housekeeper into.

"I'm in a very cross mood today," the drenched Princess Zoam said as she sat down upon Ozma's throne and found her feet didn't quite touch the floor. Her hair once naturally curly and beautiful hung around her like wet noodles and her face was very pale from the water's chill. Combined with the look of extreme anger in her eyes the first impression of many Ozites of their monarch was not a good one at all.

"Who wants to go first?" Zoam looked at the crowd of gathered Ozites and found oddly enough that none of them seemed willing.

The Wooing of Ozma
Chapter Nine

Dorothy Gale as a young woman, who had grown up considerably from the eight year old girl she had been when she was first in Oz. Yet the Kansas girl hadn't reached maidenhood despite now being a little over a hundred. Dorothy was in quite a quandary over what exactly had happened to Ozma. The Royal Princess couldn't quite put her finger on what was wrong with her best friend in the world, but whatever it was it was serious. 'Maybe she is just suffering from her crush.' Dorothy pondered as she moved through the halls of the Emerald Palace. It was hard to avoid stepping in puddles wherever one walked. It was just horrible what had been done to the place by the rain, which just didn't go away no matter how hard Dot wished it would. The house back in Kansas had occasionally sprung a leak or two but the number of them in the Palace was just ridiculous. It was then that Dorothy spotted a small figurine on the ground by Ozma's bedroom door.

"Hmmm that's funny," Dorothy said as she leaned down to pick up the small wooden toy. It looked remarkably like a miniature of the Sawhorse. Dorothy put the object in the pocket of her dress as she thought it probably belonged to some of the Emerald City children. Ozma allowed youngins to play in the palace all the time and they often scattered the toys the Wizard made for them.

"Mmmmm maybe I should talk to Betsy and Hank about what's going on."

Charles Phipps

Dorothy then remembered the pleasant girl from Oklahoma was probably caring for her Mule. The animals were getting sick the fastest here on Oz and while it was primarily small ones like Toto and the birds who were the most unwell, even the Cowardly Lion was feeling under the weather now.

"I know what's going on," The Glass Cat said, walking causally in-between Dorothy's two feet.

"Oh you do huh?" Dorothy said smiling as she picked up Doctor Pipt's creation. The Glass Cat wasn't as fun to cuddle as a normal animal because she was cold like all things glass but despite her occasionally grating personality, Dorothy still thought she was wonderful.

"Oh absolutely. I saw it all last night." The Glass Cat wagged its glass tail in Dorothy's arms.

"And what did you see?" Dorothy rubbed the glass surface above its pink marble brains. The Glass Cat smiled and looked up at Dorothy with what almost looked like a grin before it said quite clearly.

"Ozma was taken and replaced by a double." which caused Dorothy to drop the Glass Cat onto the ground where she landed with a loud thunk. Thankfully cats, even ones made out of glass, always land on their feet.

"Hummph!" the Glass Cat frowned at Dorothy. "Look at what you've done! You've chipped my tail!"

Dorothy looked at the Glass Cat's tail and noticed that there was a tiny scratch on her tail even if Dorothy could hardly call it a chip. "Glass Cat whatever do you mean that Ozma has been replaced?" despite the Princess's concern for the Glass Cat, her concern for her best friend was much greater.

The Wooing of Ozma

The Glass Cat continued looking at her tail. "I mean I'm not like the Scarecrow. It's not like my tail can be causally replaced like his straw or brains. I also want to know exactly why the Scarecrow is always about his brains. I mean it's not like you can see them work." the cat pointed to her marbles.

"Glass Cat, why didn't you tell someone earlier. You might as well have lost them if you didn't!" Dorothy frowned most testily.

"What? My heart is a ruby and very cold." the Glass Cat explained. "I saw a almost identical double of Princess Ozma bind and gag the real Princess along with another fellow whom was dressed in an ugly military uniform. She also turned the Sawhorse into a little wooden figurine which means that she can't be all bad…" The Glass Cat then noticed Dorothy was no longer paying attention to her. Having no more business with her Bungle lifted up her tail to head down to the Glass-makers to have it buffed.

Dorothy scrambled into her pocket and pulled out the miniature wooden horse. It must actually be the Sawhorse itself! "Oooooo no wonder she didn't recognize me earlier! Well that witch whoever she is isn't going to get away with it no matter what. I bet it's that Zoam person!"

Now Dorothy as you know was a very forgiving woman and not prone to rash actions but the transformation of friends into toys and the kidnapping of friends was something that she could just not stomach. No matter how often it happened. Now if she hadn't been completely angry Dorothy might have done a bit more planning than she did but Dorothy

Charles Phipps

proceeded than march herself down to the throne room to confront Princess Zoam and restore her friend.

"Oooo if they've done something Glinda can't undo I'm going to clobber her good!" Dorothy wagged her fist in the air, huffing.

***

Princess Zoam stared into the various Munchkinders and made her pronouncements, which invariably made no sense whatsoever. The Princess of Zo had learned statecraft on the knee of her father King Zozo. He had always said that people only needed a ruler so long as they couldn't think for themselves. So, the key to being a good ruler was to make sure that they remained dependant on you and your bad decisions for as long as possible. They'd been doing in America for hundreds of years successfully so Zoam certainly wasn't going to argue with the philosophy.

"That's a brilliant idea Princess Ozma! Stop making my beds and cleaning my plates altogether because they'll just get dirty again," Farmer Wendel White said. "This will show that dumb Old Farmer Brown and his walking potato crop."

"Don't forget to stop brushing your teeth as well Farmer White. Your intelligence will make you very popular socially." Princess Zoam smiled adding in her decree a wave of her wand. "Don't forget to have allot of chocolate and sweets on the way out too!"

"I won't Princess!" Farmer White waved back as he departed.

The Princess was firmly convinced that he father had been the wisest man in the universe. Of course that

The Wooing of Ozma

hadn't stopped her from turning him into a houseplant when she grew bored waiting around for a throne in an immortal countryside but that just went to show that she was even wiser than her father by her logic.

"Hello Princess Ozma!" a voice said at her feet and Princess Zoam stared at the ugly green warty face of her court jester E. Bused who was still wearing the same ridiculous costume that he wore as her fool. Princess Zoam frowned intensley and wondered what awful punishment 'Ozma' should inflict upon him as a lesson.

"Hello," The Princess said coldly.

"I've decided what form I'd like you to transform me into!" E. Bused said proudly.

"You want me to transform you?" The Princess thought that was most queer. Her mother had been an evil Fairy Queen who had passed down the knowledge of transformations so that the line of Zo could keep itself in power. After all the princible of it was turning people into objects they did NOT want to be turned into. The idea that a person could enjoy the transformation had only occurred to her yesterday when so many people she'd accidentally turned into other shapes seemed to be happy with it.

"Yes Princess, because the only thing that is truly disgusting is staying the same." E. Bused laughed and danced about. "However if I must stay the same I would like to be a seven headed wolf with a long rainbow as a tail and a spout like a whales."

Princess Zoam leveled her bronze wand at E. Bused. Zoam would have used Princess Ozma's wand but sadly the true ruler of Oz's white wands burnt her hands every time they touched her and they were impossible for to use.

"Maybe I'll turn you into a gerbil." Hopefully she could turn somebody into a big snake nearby.

"What a wonderful idea Princess! As a gerbil I could run around in a wheel for people's entertainment and be cared for as a beloved pet!" E. Bused said with a completely sincere smile that made Zoam slightly sick.

After spending most of his childhood trying to make E. Bused unhappy it just wasn't right he'd be enjoying himself now.

"Right-this-way-sir." Tik-Tok then lumbered in through the Emerald doors and past the water filled buckets. Princess Zoam turned her eyes away from her court jester and looked at the mechanical man with a unpleasant eye. Machines always made her queasy because they reminded her of Igor. Igor was a childhood playmate of hers and while she had been just learning how to change E. Bused's legs into other shapes he had been building. Igor had been building things like Tik-Tok. It made her more than a little jealous and she destroyed every machine of his that wasn't necessary for her to rule.

"Ah thank you very much most noble Mechanical Man." Milo then walked in and Princess Zoam's heart skipped a beat. The young pet mortal was everything that wasn't in Zo and while he could never understand her, the way Igor could, he had been more fun to torment than any mortal previous. Sucking in a breath she looked down at E. Bused and patted him on the head, trying to emanate Ozma's voice as best she could.

The Wooing of Ozma

"Why don't you go think about your transformation a bit more Toad man. I'm sure that with such a big decision you'll want to think heavily about it." Zoam then shook off the slime that came onto her hand with the best smile she could give. It was the kind of smile children give to Dentists when they are inside your mouth and not a very realistic one at all.

E. Bused accepted it joyfully and bounced off though because Toads are not reknowned for their vision.

"Your-Ro-yal-High-ness. I-have-brought-the-prisoner-who-was-found-in-the-act-of-woo-ing." Tik Tok rumbled and pointed to Milo. Tik Tok had generously allowed the man to change into a new suit for the occasion of his trial which of course was another one of his identical Sunday ones.

"Oh is that a crime in Oz?" Zoam asked. When she was new to maidenhood many young men of Zo had tried to court her but when they played off key she had turned them into kudzo for her castle. Eventually they had stopped coming so she had made it a law that every attractive young man in Zo had to woo her every night or join them growing on her castle. The only problem with that is it had led to a shortage of attractive young men in Zo.

"Yes-Your-Majesty," Tik Tok said without the least problem repeating himself to his princess. "Milo-would-you-mind-winding-me-up? I-think-my-actions-and-thoughts-are-about-to-run-down."

"Oh certainly." Milo leaned in before Ozma put her wand in front of his helping hands.

"Oh that won't be necessarily Milo My Dear." Zoam smiled batting her eyelashes happily at him.

113

Charles Phipps

"Ummm well Princess I think it's best. Polychrome taught me all..." Milo adjusted his Oz clothes for a moment and said. "Princess you'll forgive me of trying to woo you but in the time that I have come to know you I think."

Princess Zoam was completely ignoring the fact the young Preacher to be was talking about Ozma and not her. The Usurper leaned into his arms and looked deeply into his eyes. "Oh really Milo? I never knew you cared so much about me."

Milo looked at 'Ozma' and discovered that something was most mysteriously wrong with the woman he had fallen in love with. Instead of the warm caring woman that he had seen in her eyes he instead saw a person with a vain, selfish, and quite unattractive spirit. Before the young man could put two and two together. Specifically Ozma he loved and Zoam he did not + Ozma was a good person and this person was not, there was a crashing at the door.

"Stop right there you...you...wanton woman you!" Dorothy Gale shouted at the top of her lungs as she threw open the Emerald doors. Zoam watched Tik-Tok run down even as she grabbed Milo by the throat and held her wand to the side of his head. "Don't move or your little handsome prince here is going to become a hideous amphibian!'

"I resemble that remark," The Frogman to one side said with as much indignity as he could with being unable to tell any untruths. You of course can imagine how confusing it must have been for the average citizen of Oz to wonder why their ruler was threatening Beloved Princess Dorothy and a inoffensive man in his Sunday clothes.

The Wooing of Ozma

"Zoam!" Milo says looking up and finally finishing the mathematical equation we described earlier... which of course only explained the situation to E. Bused and Raspy. Both of whom had come to the court of Ozma for various reasons and both of which were quite petrified by the presence of their ex-ruler.

***

The Wizard of Oz had been trying all day to figure out just how to repair the holes in the roof that had started because of this confounded rainstorm. It should have been simplicity for a very powerful Wizard to figure out how to magick up a solution but in the end the problems just became worse. A very intelligent man, the Wizard had gladly deferred to Uncle Henry in this matter. The Farmer's solution was having a much better effect than all the spells, potions, and concoctions that Oscar had brewed up to fix the Emerald Palace. It just went to show even a not-humbug wizard was the solution to everything. Waiting to speak with Princess Ozma about requesting a hundred gallons of tar from the Gillikens he was shocked when the situation with Dorothy, the nice young wooer he was setting up with Ozma, and obviously the false princess from Zo enfolded before him. 'I need to do something and something fast before that woman turns us all into grape jelly.' The Wizard thought then stepped forward in a dramatic rush. "Ah ha! Princess Zoam! Do you honestly think my dear Dorothy would come here without considerable backup? No matter what shape you could turn that poor boy into we have powers that could easily break the enchantment!" the Wizard decided to play his cards where they lay, which meant he was going to lie a great deal in hopes he wasn't caught.

"Mister Diggs what exactly are you doing?" Milo said understandably reluctant to do anything with a wand of transformation to his forehead.

"You don't frighten me Wizard of Oz. I'll have you know I have the Wishing Belt on me and if I wanted I could make this entire countryside into mindless slaves who…who…" Zoam tried to find a nasty image but even rainy Oz was so nice it was hard to concentrate.

"Ah, but I've cast a magical spell on the Wishing Belt Zoam that prevents anyone evil from ever using it." Oz gave a sign with his fingers behind his back towards Dorothy who moved to the side. Of course it was a complete lie, putting a magical spell on the magic of whatever force had created the Wishing Belt was well beyond his power or even Glinda's but the art of a showman was to appear to have powers beyond those that they understood. Then again the art of a showman wouldn't help him if he was a billy goat but the Wizard was under the impression Zoam wasn't the swiftest duck in the flock.

"Your lying and I'll prove it now!" Zoam rose up even as Oz signalled the Toad man. "Jump man! Grab her!"

E. Bused the Toad wasn't sure what to do. On one hand he had made some fine friends in the short time he had been in Oz but on the other hand he was very afraid of Princess Zoam and what she might turn him into. Still, Easily reasoned, it was better he get turned into something unpleasant than the nice people who

The Wooing of Ozma

probably weren't as used to being transformed as he was.

"Gotcha Princess!" E. Bused leapt up on Princess Zoam's head even as Milo grabbed at her wand. Zoam went tumbling to the ground under the weight of the giant toad and her power source went sailing on the ground, right until Dorothy grabbed right it up. With a smile Dorothy tapped it on the Sawhorse figurine which was restored in an instant to its proper if extremely annoyed form.

"Ooooo wait until I get Ozma's wand to her! You nasty folk you!" the Sawhorse said then realized that he in the palace throne room.

"Get the Wishing Belt my boy!" Oz said with a smile, a plan of his actually working for once. "I think it is time we had a chat with the unpleasant Magical Monarch of Zo."

"Oooo I'll get you all for this!" Zoam cried but bereft of her wand the evil fairy's magic was very weak indeed.

Chapter Ten

Princess Ozma looked at the Black Spectacled Order with a great deal of pity as she thought about her plan to escape. It was a plan that required Igor's father to have not been too careful with his enchantment of those spectacles. Still, she guessed any man who would design such horrid magic as them couldn't have been too serious about his magic.

"ARE YOU READY SNARK SNARK?" Princess Ozma shouted at the top of her lungs. She'd already discovered the Guard's magic earmuff's heard whispers as shouts so she presumed that they would hear whispers when she shouted.

"ABSOLUTELY PRINCESS OZMA!" the Snark Snark shouted at the top of his lungs which were huge. The result which was fairly deafening but none of the Black Spectacled Order moved an inch from their positions or even seemed to take notice.

Princess Ozma then sat down in her cage and looked at the Snark Snark with her back turned to the Black Spectacled Order and then said very quietly in the Snark Snark's direction. "It worked! You've almost got the makeshift key to work! We'll soon be free."

"Ah ha!" the leader of the Black Spectacled Order (Whose name was Phil) whispered at the bottom of his lungs that Ozma had to strain to hear the man. "You underestimate us hideous Princess Ozma of the Ozites. We've heard every last thing you've just said. Gregor go tighten the Snark Snark's lock!"

The Wooing of Ozma

Ozma smiled broadly which must have appeared as a terrible frown to the Black Spectacled Guard. One of the guards whom she presumed to be Gregor then brought over a heavy lead key to the Snark Snark's chains where he promptly inserted the key and turned it, freeing the Snark Snark.

"Princess Ozma!" The Snark Snark shouted, tossing upwards the key from his chains to her cage as the Princess caught the lead key and she turned it in the cold iron cage's lock. It was hard work but with a single turn she was able to free herself from her prison and leap out onto the back of the invisible Snark Snark. The great beast rose upwards in the dungeon and soon it towered over the Black Spectacled Order like a skyscrapper.

"Help! Help! The Crone and her monster have escaped! Get the canons! Get the catapults! Get the dynamite! Get me out of here!" Phil the Leader ran around as his own men did roughly the same thing. Because the Snark Snark was invisible they had no idea what it actually look like and they had very good idea it was something terrible. In truth no one actually knows what a Snark Snark looks like, least of all themselves. But, from what people who have encountered them know, they probably look like big furry elephants and are not terrifying at all.

Seeing that the Black Spectacled Order were getting weapons Ozma decided to put a stop to this little encounter before it got dangerous. "Upsey Daisyus Wygotyxxius!" Ozma did one of the few spells in her posession that didn't require her wand and the Guard's magical glasses and earmuffs promptly flew off their heads.

119

Charles Phipps

The effect was immediate on the guardsman who once removed of their magical prisons wondered exactly what was wrong with everything. First of all you must realize that the guards had been wearing their glasses and earmuffs for a long time and had forgotten just what handsome chaps they were when they were removed. Also the sudden transformation from Ozma the hideous crone to Ozma the beautiful princess made them silent with awe.

"What should we do now?" the Snark Snark asked Ozma.

Ozma however knew exactly what to do. Sliding down the Snark Snark's trunk before the soldiers of Zo she presented herself "I am Ozma rightful ruler of Oz and monarch of all lands that bear its flag! You who have imprisoned me have committed a great crime against your sister country and for that I vow to remove my cousin Queen Zo from power." it was a terrible oath but Ozma didn't think Zoam deserved such a title after what she had done.

Phil and the rest of the Black No-longer Spectacled Order looked at Ozma and weighed their loyalty to their queen.

"Well fine by me," Phil said.

"I never really much cared for her anyway." Gregor answered as well.

Ozma nodded then gestured to the lead key. "Then as your new ruler I command you to go forward and release all my wrongfully imprisoned subjects! I shall prepare to remove the wicked from their positions and lead them to freedom. I'll also need your help friend Snark Snark in finding the Weather Machine of Igor. Does your nose work well?" the legends of the Snark

The Wooing of Ozma ·

Snark's ability to find storms was quite popular in Oz, along with the legend of the Silly Oz...something she forgot what they were called, and the Woozy.

"Enough to find the heart of this thunderstorm," the Snark Snark said while thunder clapped outside and echoed through the dungeon.

"Excellent. Can you ferry me on your back?" Princess Ozma asked and thenchuckled lightly as she was lifted by its' hairy trunk onto its furry spine.

"Of course Your Highness." the Snark Snark smiled.

It was not long after that Phil and the other Dungeon guards had released the prisoners of Oz and while a few of the Kalidahs, Flesh Eating Skrewgs, and Fire Breathing Krugs were troublesome Ozma was able to keep them in line by sheer virtue of her authority as Mistress of Oz. Forming them into a parade like procession, Ozma proceeded to march the First Oz Army of Conquest up the stairs into the palace of Zo and destiny.

***

Princess Zoam was forcefully fed three spoonfuls of the Wizard of Oz's 'Patented Gumdrop Flavored Magic Removing St. John's Wort Paste' and locked away in the Palace prison-room, which was the wonderfully comfortable room Milo had left. Everyone in the Palace was extremely worried. Ozma had been kidnapped before but the damage already done to Oz by the Weather makers of Zo showed they were a powerful adversary. Furthermore whenever Ozma left Oz it seemed to get weaker and its troubles much worse, the best country in the universe couldn't stand much more of these troubles.

"Oh dear whatever are we going to do?" Dorothy paced around the room until she spotted the Good Witch of the South entering through the front door of the Throneroom.

"We're going to rescue Her Majesty obviously," E. Bused said. The Toad Jester was feeling awfully proud of himself since his help in the defeat of the Ozma imposter and was doing backflips and standing on his head as a bizzare way to celebrate.

"I think our dear sweet Dorothy means that we need to know how we will rescue Ozma not whether or not we will," The Wizard said crossing his arms and leaning back.

"Oh yes that makes perfect sense. Sorry." E. Bused put a webbed finger to his mouth and nodded.

"Jellia Jamb has already told me about the situation Wizard. I must say it is rather dire but not insurmountable. Unfortunately they've already stolen my Book of Records and finding clues to where is will be problematic indeed." Glinda said causally. In Glinda's left hand was a very pretty pink umbrella, which magically kept those under it warm and dry. It had been a gift from the rather lovesick U.N Fold some time ago. To her side was Jellia and an extremely wet but well-oiled Tin Woodsman.

"These Zoites seem like they've got us outsmarted at every turn." Dorothy frowned heavily.

"Overpowered Dorothy yes…at least at first. Surprised…oh certainly. Outsmarted? Never." Glinda waved her wand a bit in the air.

The Wooing of Ozma

"The Princessssssssssss Ozma will ccccccertainly be located in the palaccccccce of Zo Lady Glinda. Unfortunately if Igor Lackey hassssssss managed to bring up the country'sssssss defenssssssessss then it will be almosssssssst imposssssssible for anyone to penetrate them alive." Raspy the Hissing Wing spoke from his memories as the Captain of the Guard of Zo. The country of the Weather Makers was only invaded three times before people stopped believing it had anything worth taking. Each time, those involved directly in attacking Zo were utterly destroyed.

"Hmmm do we let the dead in causally?" E. Bused asked what he thought was a very sensible question.

"Igor Lackey? Of the Winkie Lackeys?" Glinda asked her next question with a good deal of shock.

"You've heard of this fella?" Dorothy asked Glinda.

"The Winkie Lackeys are the children of the Wicked Witch of the West and their descendants. They are without a doubt the vilest group of necromancers, alchemists, warlocks, and witches that have ever lived in Oz. When Evile Lackey the Machinist devised a potion so vile that it put the entire country of Oz at threat, I drove the entire family and their minions away." Glinda frowned thinking that the attack on Oz may have other motives and of course being right. "If one of them is involved I do not believe they will be simply satisfied trading their ruler for ours." The words were considerably disheartening to all.

"I don't see why they'd want her back either," The Glass Cat murmured as she sat underneath the Sawhorse. The Wizard looked at the cat crossly. A large number of Oz's residents were very angry with

Charles Phipps

the Glass Cat for not telling them sooner about Ozma's kidnapping.

Milo Trustworthy Starling meanwhile was sitting in one corner thinking.

Everyone in the room was feeling Ozma's loss and while he had not known her like Dorothy or Glinda for a century he felt keenly this loss. Because indeed Milo loved her and could think of only the pain she would be feeling at her friend's worrying about her. It was then that Milo hatched upon a plan that had he not been desperate to save the Princess he might have seen a few holes in.

"Eureka!" Milo stood up straight and looked directly at Glinda the Good Witch of the South.

"No, down here," Eureka the Cat said.

"No I'm sorry I didn't mean you." Milo said. Eureka of course meaning also "I have found it."

"Hmmmmph." Eureka frowned and went over to stand by her best friend and rival the Glass Cat.

"If Raspy the Hissing Wing knows the defenses of Zo and there are others who know the City streets and Palace layout…E. Bused and myself." Milo didn't know them well he admitted to himself but he had seen them. "Then it is possible I suspect for a man on a single creature's back to maneuver past their defenses, go into the palace proper, and knock out their magical weapon." the young preacher said.

"Are you sure that will work?" Dorothy asked concerned.

"It did in Star Wars," Milo said as he adjusted his Sunday tie.

Sadly the movie was not very popular in Oz and the reference did not do much to assuage them.

The Wooing of Ozma

"Forgive me Mister Starling but are you suggesting we allow you to go on this mission alone?"

"The best equipped army cannot save a king for great strength is not enough to save anyone." Milo said openly. "Substitute Princess for King and it says openly much about the chances of others. Lady Glinda I fear I have fallen deeply in love with your ruler and no matter how high a mountain must I climb, how deep a valley I must dig, how great a foe I must face if she is in danger I will gladly put myself to it for her sake."

"Sniff. That's beautiful," Sir Hokus said wiping a tear from his eye.

"Courage is no insurance of success Sir Starling nor any guarantee of Our Lady's feelings." Glinda not too gently reminded him.

"Not to mention you might have asked us about this before volunteering us." E. Bused pointed out.

Milo looked at them. "Oh sorry about that."

"No problem." E. Bused waved and Rapsy gave a claws up to his master.

"I seek nothing from Her Majesty Lady Glinda. Not even the right to woo her as Sir Tik Tok has rather plainly stated is against the law here in the Merry Old Land of Oz," Milo went on before the Scarecrow could point out it was not so Merry right now. "However I would very much like to help and I am willing to make whatever sacrifices are necessary to ensure success. Providence may well have put me here to make them to keep the Lady Ozma from losing a truer friend."

"What'd he say?" E. Bused asked Polychrome who was standing to one side.

"I think he said Ozma would be less upset if he got turned into something unpleasant than say Dorothy."

Charles Phipps

Polychrome added. "Which just isn't true!" she said with a huff.

Glinda nodded towards the man as she was satisfied with his answer. Ozma was rather like a daughter to the Good Witch of the South who had no offspring of her own and she was protective of her. Still, Glinda's magical truth sensing pearl registered the sincerity of the man's words and she bade him to approach. "Pick up your umbrellas Sir, that U.N. Fold has made for you."

Milo gathered up the seven umbrellas which he'd laid beside Ozma's throne as Glinda placed an enchantment on each. "The Umbrellas will shrink to pocket size until you require them. I have given each a magical trait that can be used on your quest. I fear to say that Oz will not be able to stand many more of these storms and if you do not succeed within a day we will make our own preparations to restore Oz."

Some say it might have been cruel of Glinda not to tell Milo that in a day the Magic Belt would be recharged and they could simply say "I wish Ozma restored to us and Zo far far away" to put an end to this but she felt that she was doing something to help the onset of love.

Milo bowed to Glinda and got on the back of the Raspy as E. Bused clutched hold of the Hissing Wing's feet and they set into the air out of the nearest balcony.

"Well now that that's settled, who wants lunch?" the Wizard said with a smile.

***

Igor Lackey sat in his laboratory pouring over the Book of Records his minions had placed here for his

The Wooing of Ozma

reading. The volume was immense and held more in it than could ever be adequately read by a normal human being but Igor wasn't skimming for the secrets of Oz this time but looking solely for information about his beloved Zoam.

"The Princess of Zo is betrayed by her court Jester E. Bused and locked away in prison by the Wizard of Oz." the words rather clearly stated and Igor searched for references to Glinda who had so callously driven out his family from Oz years before.

Igor looked up at the iron bottle potion that his father made over a century ago. The dusty bottle hadn't been touched in the entire time it had rested in Zo since his father's disappearance and Igor feared to touch it. If worse came to worse the Weather-Maker of Zo might use it to threaten Oz but that was definitely a last resort and only if he could not get his precious Princess back any other way. Igor did not have any moral quams about using the terrifying magic in the bottle but it was so powerful it might destroy him just as surely as it might an enemy. It was that that moment Igor found the reference he was looking for in the immense Book of Records.

"Glinda the Good Witch of the South then charged Milo Starling with invading the land of Zo with the magical tools she gave him."

Igor looked at that particular passage. Then he looked at it again. Then re-read it to make sure that he had seen it right. Finally Igor shook the book to make sure it hadn't malfunctioned. "That witch is sending a mortal to attack our beautiful..." a few drops of water landed on Igor's head from the steaming, bubbling,

Charles Phipps

and thoroughly ugly machinery behind him. "Kingdom?

Obviously these tools must be very powerful or she expects him to utterly fail."

Igor then got a most terrible plan, which was pretty much the entire sum of the types of plans he had I'm sorry to say.

"Agatha!" Igor called his Harpy mother down again. The evil monster appeared just a few moments later as she ran through the door.

"Yes my son?" the hideous crone with her sharp teeth looked at her son. Her eyes were beady and like black-eyed peas instead of the normal eyes you or eye have had since birth. Her feathers were dirty and dark from living in the filthy confines of Zo and her breath was none too pleasant either.

However because Agatha the Harpy was still a mother we should respect her nonetheless.

"The mortal you captured earlier Milo, the one who escaped. He is going to be coming to Zo very soon and I want you to ignore the Princess's orders to take him back alive. Since no one can be killed in this accursed land I want you to tear him to pieces and place them in the four quadrants of this land or toss them in the Deadly Desert!" Igor's wrath was most fierce because he could not stand that even for a moment someone else could attract his Princess's attention. The fact that Milo Starling was not a fairy or a wizard made him even more angry because Igor did not respect anyone who did not have magic in their veins.

The Wooing of Ozma

Agatha smiled because Harpies like doing such things "As is your pleasure my son." and flew into the air to attack the heroes already in quite a bit of danger.

Chapter Eleven

Ozma rode on the Snark Snark's back down the bleak dungeon corridors and decided that the direct way was probably not a good idea to go this route through the dungeon. Despite this being the route the guards had suggested (or because of it), it was not really suitable for their march. While there were steps directly up into the palace of Zo, the doors were just too small for quite a few of the Oz inhabitants that Ozma had to lead home. Phil the leader of the now Spectacle-Less Order (also known as the First Revolutionary Council of Zo) insisted that the tunnels they were presently following would lead them up to the heart of the Obsidian City. Ozma supposed she could have transformed all the large creatures into smaller ones but she had never been very good at shrinking and after seeing her beloved Sawhorse transformed earlier, the Princess decided that it would best if they avoided such altogether.

"However did you get so much obsidian?" Ozma asked looking at the lava-glass walls and tunnels that were ever present. It seemed almost a parody of the Emerald City that the Wizard had built but that was many years after Zo had departed Oz.

"When Zo was still part of Oz it was originally just a beautiful kingdom of clouds Your Majesty but eventually one of King Zo's descendants decided he wanted a fairy bride. He fell in love with the daughter of Vulcan the Forger. To make her more comfortable the King insisted they steal a volcano from the Earth so Zo could be as hot as the fiery furnace that was her

The Wooing of Ozma

home. So much obsidian was made by the constant meeting of lava and water that we eventually just started building the entire city out of it. The Kingdom of Zo now reflects their daughter Princess Zoam's personality perfectly, constantly rumbling about something and steaming." Phil the Revolutionary Council leader informed the Princess. The Guard Captain was still dressed in Black Spetacled Guard uniform, sans the spetacles and earmuffs of course, but Ozma had assured him he could get a new uniform soon. His uniform really was hideous but the Captain had liked it alot when he had been wearing his glasses.

"How awful," Princess Ozma said, imagining it.

"If you think that's bad try and imagine what it feels like to live here!

Constantly humid, everyone is always having a bad day and complaining about it until nobody cares to hear it any longer. It's twice as bad for the old so they're twice as nasty because they hurt so much. Its' no wonder everyone in Zo is so rotten." Phil the Revolutionary Council leader nodded before all of his soldiers on the Council gave a hearty "here here" behind him.

"Well bad weather is no excuse for being mean I can assure you that the days of suffering in Zo are over," Ozma informed as she rode resolute in her purpose.

"Stop you ugly fairy woman type person you!" A rather unpleasant voice rang out through the dark and dismal caverns.

"Oh dear I hope this isn't more of the Black Spectacled Guard." The Snark Snark murmured.

Charles Phipps

"They'd have to be milady to think you are ugly," Phil said before brushing his hair and looking at Ozma. Ozma gave him a frown to remind him he was happily married though how long that would remain so, because he had been so under the magical glasses and earmuffs, was anyone's guess.

Ozma got off the Snark Snark's neck and then walked up to see where the voice had come from. "Pardon me sir but why should we stop?" It was then that the ruler of Oz came across a truly grizzly sight.

Row after row of heads on pedestals were resting in front of the tunnel. The heads included both male and female with many of them wearing the inverted crown of Oz that Ozma had discovered was the symbol of Zo. Ozma noticed to her shock that aside from the few among the faces who were obesely fat and contorted with obscene cruelty, that they mostly bore the features of the Royal House of Oz!

"We the Royal Family of Zo command it!" one of the heads shouted He a long thick black mustache and eyebrows which made his sneer most menacing.

"And more specifically because I the greatest of Zo's Queens, Zoette the Beautiful do," a rather unnattractive woman with her nose curled in the air said.

"HA! I was the most beautiful of Zo's queens and my husband Zoar the Destroyer was the cruelest as well," a more attractive but still pignosed young woman with the Zo crown on her head revived.

"Oh be quiet Zoia. I am King Zo the First and Superior to all of you! If you wish to pass this tunnel you must bow down and pay homage to the Lord of Zo Island!" The biggest head of them all was a man whom

The Wooing of Ozma

Ozma was surprised to say looked remarkably like her grandfather Ozroar. He was crosseyed however with one eye bloodshot and twisted and the other looking around frantically for something.

"Why are you all down here?" Ozma couldn't hide her surprise at seeing a large number of decapitated royals in the dungeon. Still, the Princess had not lost her wits and she certainly was not going to pay homage to such a silly group. A ruler had her pride you know.

"In a tradition started by my son..." The First King of Zo looked accusingly toward a head that looked very much like him. "The monarchs of Zo have always chopped off the heads of their parents when they think it is time for them to ascend the throne. Because of a magical spell placed on the Royal Family however we do not die and thus we were stored in the most regal section of Zo to give our wisdom to them."

"Like how to steal from the peasants and not get caught!" King Zoar the Destroyer shouted heartily.

"And how to chop off your parent's heads when we get bored with just each other!" Zoette pointed out.

"I see," Ozma said, trying to hide her repulsion.

"That is until Zoam," King Zo the First actually spat at Ozma's feet after saying Zoam's name.

"Aiye, Zoam!" the other monarchs followed suit spitting and Ozma had to hide behind the Snark Snark to avoid getting hit.

"It would appear the current ruler of Zo is not even very popular with the former tyrants of our land Princess Ozma." Phil lifted up his obsidian spear, which Ozma had insisted he take the point off of lest he hurt someone.

Charles Phipps

"Princess Zoam not only didn't decapitate her father in the proper Zoam fashion but she didn't even do anything to her mother period!" Prince Zorg who had been sadly de-bodied by his father while trying to de-body him said woefully.

"Not to mention that she moved us down from our beautifully richly appointed display room to this cold drafty dungeon!" Zoia said looking around the dirty obsidian tunnel and admittadly Ozma had to agree that it was not a very nice place for even a head to rest in.

"Wait, did you say your name was Ozma?" King Zo the First said.

"No Sir Phil my servant said my name was Ozma but it is truly my name," Ozma corrected. "And my status as the ruler of Oz is the reason I will not bow down and pay you homage. I think your fate very appropriate for the way you have mistreated your subjects and families by your own words." Ozma said with as much dignity as she could muster and that was quite a bit.

"Then by our royal authority you shall not pass!" King Zo said to a resounding agreement behind him.

"You know Princess Ozma I don't think there is exactly much that they could do to stop us." The Snark Snark said lifting Ozma with his trunk back onto his neck.

Now being heads without bodies or magic to call their own the Kings and Queens of Zo decided then to resort to the only weapon they had left in excessive taunting. Ozma ignored her cousins and many greats removed Uncle as they said things about her looks, intelligence, and upbringing which were not true but hurt nonthless. The procession proceeded past the

The Wooing of Ozma

heads with the only real incident a young Munchkin boy kicking over the pedestal King Zo was on and letting his head roll away.

"As much as they are a rude, crude, and monstrous group of people I don't like leaving them down there in that Dungeon Your Highness," Phil said as he walked by the Snark Snark's side with his spear as a staff.

"For all of their evil Phil they are still family to me and I will remove them from this place when it is all done. I simply have no desire to listen to their complaints until this island is safely under the flag of Oz." Ozma smiled at the thought of curing all of the evil in Zo. A task that the ruler was soon to find a much more difficult task than she had originally expected.

***

Milo Starling held tightly to the back of the Hissing Wing and sucked in his breath. For the ride upwards through the rain was not smoothe in the slightest and Milo was mildly acrophobic. Aside from a few instances where Milo had ridden in an airplane he'd never been flying before and I can assure you riding in an airplane is quite different than riding bare back on a creature known for it's love of crashing in the middle of a rainstorm!

"RIBBBBBBBIIIIITTTT!" E. Bused said at the top of his lungs while his webbed hands clutched around the legs of Raspy. If Milo was having trouble with his ride he had reason to be grateful he wasn't in his companion's position.

Charles Phipps

Truth be told it wasn't that pleasant for Raspy either ferrying two men through the air. Worse, two heavy men who didn't like crashing.

"There Zo is! I can see the outer towers!" Milo shouted past the thundering rainstorm. The young hero pointed to the twisted obsidian walls that marked the edge of the clouds of Zo. Even so far away, the dull black and whites of Zo were a bleak contrast to the vibrant multicolored land of Oz below.

"Exccccccccellent! Now all we have to do isssssssss get passssssssst the entire flying guard of Zo!" Raspy said smiling. No sooner had he finished saying it then out of the towers started pouring dozens and dozens of hideous monsters. The harpies, half women and half birds were Zo's vanguard. It should be noted contrary to popular mythology the majority of harpies are actually quite beautiful, musically inclined folk with a strong cultural tradition. It just so happened that these harpies were the exception to the rule being ugly, mean, and their strong cultural tradition being toward cannibalism. The horde screeched as they descended toward the small group in droves.

"Oh dear. This doesn't look good," Milo cried with a wince.

"Don't worry it getsssssssss much worssssssssse! They can also toss fireballs!" Raspy said with a smile. Hissing-Wings, aside from crashing,

enjoy danger and that shows why they so often become heroes outside of Zo, a place where they are predominately minions of evil. But you knew that.

The sky soon was lit up like a fireworks show as the Harpy's withdrew balls of fire from their mouth and began to toss them down.

The Wooing of Ozma

"I'd get out those magic umbrellas if I were you. Wooaaaaaaaaaaaaah!" E. Bused shouted even as Raspy ducked in-between the fireballs as best he could.

"Oh blast it. I probably should have found out what they did first! Ala-kazam!" Milo lifted up the first umbrella he picked out of his pocket and shouted the only magical word he knew. Of course that magical word requires a top-hat and a wand to summon a rabbit but thankfully the red umbrella's magic didn't require a word to activate.

"Aiyeeeee! I'm on fire!" One of the harpies screeched as more harpies joined the chorus. The Red Umbrella Glinda had enchanted to be protection against fire and as so many fireballs rained down on the umbrella they proceedex promptly to bounce right back up at those who threw them.

"Good job massssssssster! Do you want ussssss to crasssssh now?" Rapsy said back as Milo whacked each fireball in turn like a baseball would a ball.

"Let's take a rain check on that! Get it? Haha I kill me!" E. Bused said up to Rapsy. The Toadman very nearly spoke the truth as his toad legs just barely missed being taken off by a fireball.

"If we can avoid crashing at this point Raspy I'd very much appreciate it." Milo held as strong as he could with his left hand to the hissing wing even as he batted the fireballs away from him and when he could back at the Harpies. Within a few minutes all of the monstrous bird women were on fire but Agatha. The first defense worse of Zo with their wings burned were sent sailing downwards to Oz in defeat. The majority once they recovered from their fall promptly gave up flight and went on to live normal productive lives as travelling muscians. Agatha herself had no desire to attack a hissing wing captain however or young Milo with his magical umbrella and flew out of their way. The Harpy Queen wouldn't have made a good travelling muscian anyway.

"Hissss! We'll get them in the city proper with the slavercruds!" Agatha shouted even as she remembered her son's defenses of the City Gates and gave a twisted smile. The Harpy Queen did not believe that the small group would survive the city despite having downed forty of her sisters, daughters, and grandchildren. It was a thought that gave the evil monster considerable pleasure.

Milo, Raspy, and E. Bused reached the City Gates of Zo then as a strong gust of wind blew into Rapsy's wings and sent the Hissing Wing Captain sailing into a tumble that dumped them right at the foot of the Obsidian city's entrance. At the City of Zo's entrance there were two hundred foot tall black doors of iron that were cold, coarse, and emblazoned with the symbol of Zo. To each door's side was an identical two hundred foot tall giant made of stone. The menacing features of their faces were chiseled on rather than grown like your face or mine.

"Oooooooph," Raspy exclaimed landing in a thump on E. Bused.

"Ughhhhhhh," E. Bused said having a several hundred pound Hissing Wing on his back.

"Oh my," Milo muttered on top and he was gentlemanly enough to get off and help the other two back up to their feet.

"That was a wonderful crash." Rapsy sighed then the Hissing Wing stopped for a moment to think about

The Wooing of Ozma

what he just said. "I must have hit my head in that crash because I don't slur my s's anymore. Well how about that!"

"The good man can look forward to happiness while the wicked can expect only wrath! We've done it my friends! We've breached Zo! Now all we have to do is rescue Princess Oz..." Milo quoted another passage before he was shook by a heavy booming voice and nearly fell off Zo's edge.

"WHO DARES APPROACH THE GATES OF THE CURSED LAND OF ZO? IF YOUR BUSINESS IS OF GOOD INTENT, PREPARE YE FOR DOOM!" One of the Stone Giants said in a very low monotone voice which nevertheless was among the loudest things that Milo had ever heard.

"Oh my, it's a golem. One of the magical creations of wizards animated by elemental spirits to defend places important to them," Milo said looking on in shock before E. Bused gave him a curious look. "Oh sorry you just have to know these kind of things if you are going to be a minister."

Milo began thumbing through his pockets for an umbrella that might help him in this situation when the other golem walked forward and leaned down to look at Milo.

"I AM KA. MY BROTHER BOOM AND I HAVE ORDERS TO SQUOOSH YOU IF YOU DO NOT INTEND HARM. DO YOU INTEND HARM?" The golem looked at Milo as his voice was almost a gushing wind.

"Well if we do intend harm will you let us pass?" Milo asked. He was in a very dear spot because he really didn't intend harm for anyone and just wanted to

Charles Phipps

free the beautiful Lady Ozma from her imprisonment. Despite being kidnapped, imprisoned in a dungeon, and generally mistreated by an overly affectionate Zoam, Milo really had nothing against the Zo people. Milo also wasn't going to lie because of his promise to Ozma even if it might have helped in the situation.

Ka then lifted up and walked over to Boom where they began to whisper to each other. Of course their whispers were still very audible shouts but it was just Golem talk and like Milo's singing I'm sure of no interest to the reader whatsoever.

"Do you think any of your magical umbrellas will help in this situation Master?" Raspy asked though his name wasn't very appropriate anymore.

"I'm not sure and I'm rather hesitant to try out," Milo admitted picking up the blue umbrella. He perhaps should have asked Glinda what the things did before he took off to rescue Ozma. Men did foolish things when they were in love though and that was part of why love was so interesting.

"WE'RE NOT SURE!" Ka then said. "SO IF YOU MEAN HARM WE THINK WE SHOULD SQUOOSH YOU TOO."

"I was afraid they were going to say that." E. Bused murmured and then flicked another fly into his mouth. Milo then slapped E. Bused on the back of the head, causing him to spit the fly out.

"That could be somebody's mother for all we know," Milo said before he exclaimed "Wait a second!"

Boom, who had lifted his foot above the trio and was about to squash them flat, stopped. "YES?"

The Wooing of Ozma

"What if we don't mean harm but are going to cause it anyway?" Milo questioned, counting on Golems not being the smarest of magical constructs.

That honor of course belonging to the Scarecrow of Oz then Bungle the Cat whose brains you can see work.

Boom walked back to talk to his brother Ka about whether that meant they should squoosh them or not.

"That was a rather clever trick." E. Bused smiled before doing a backflip and pulling out some multicolored balls to juggle.

"Unfortunately I don't think it will buy us much more time. A wise man thinks ahead, a fool doesn't and these two don't strike me as the wisest of beings. Well we had best try out this umbrella while we still have the chance then I guess." Milo unfolded the blue umbrella. In a swoosh Milo nearly let go of it as a tornado appeared out of the folds of it and began to spin the three of them in the air, over the walls and into the city of Zo. The three invaders of the Island of Zo where not even noticed by the huge golems as they flew by.

"WE'VE DECIDED TO SQUOOSH YOU," Ka said looking down where he expected to find the trio but of course found nothing. The golem scratched his head before beginning another argument with his brother.

Inside the city walls Milo, E. Bused, and Raspy landed with a thump in the middle of the Slavercrud's Castle roof.

Chapter Twelve

The Slavercrud's Castle was one of the more unpleasant monuments in Zo for our heroes as well as one of the more bizarre. It's architect Rainfeld the Mad had decided that the Slavercruds, being a flying race, would be better able to access the streets to perform their duties by building the Castle upside down. In time, the Slavercruds would come to live with the Harpies and the Hissing Wings and the Castle would become an even more unpleasant place than simply a building where all the plumbing was upside down.

"I REALLY DO HATE FLYINGGGGGGGG!" Milo shouted before slamming face first into a tumbling skid on the dungeon of the Castle, which was of course also the roof.

"Another crash! Yesssssssssss!" Rapsy smiled hitting behind Milo into another tumble.

E. Bused merely covered his eyes as he landed on his feet with the tornado propelling him setting down the Toad Man quite gently.

"Boy that was lucky." E. Bused smiled before the Blue Umbrella came flying down and clonked the Toad clean on the head, knocking him out.

"That putsssssss me at twenty ssssssssseven thoussssssand sssssssix hundred sssssucesssssssful crasssssshesssss!" Raspy hissed with a smile then frowned.

"Curssssessss, I've regained my lisssssssssp."

Milo, checking his teeth one by one to make sure he still had them all,

The Wooing of Ozma

walked over to Rapsy and shook his head. "Well I'm sorry to hear that my friend. A few flaws never hurt anyone because it is written 'Proud men end in shame but the meek become wise'." Milo then examined the roof of the upside down Slavercrud home and saw the Zo skyline which included Igor's evil looking Tower and the Obsidian Palace that Milo (wrongly) presumed held Ozma prisoner.

"I'd rather avoid wisssssdom if it were all the sssssame to you Masssster." Rapsy smiled getting up.

"And why is that?" Milo asked as he checked E. Bused to make sure that the Toadman was alright.

"Then I couldn't enjoy crassssssshing. I'd alsssssssso be too sssssmart to enjoy thisssssss crazy quessssst," Rapsy said as he sniffed the air.

"I must admit I find that logic fairly hard to argue with. However since we are now in Zo I suggest we devote our efforts to finding Princess Ozma. My heart skips a beat every time I think about what terrible fate might befalling her." Milo remembered the prison of Zo quite well and would rather have stayed there a thousand years than Ozma suffer it for one minute. It was quite a sick painful feeling in the bottom of his stomach that Milo couldn't shake away. It was then that the young began to wrinkle his nose as well.

"Egad, that's an awful smell." Milo pinched his nose as Rapsy looked at him.

"Tis the Sssssslavercrudsssss." Rapsy said with a wiggling beak.

"They're probably coming to eat your toes and faces. Thankfully I have no toes!" E. Bused said merrily wiggling his flippers as he got up and shook his head. "Though I don't suppose I'd enjoy my face being eaten off either.

I wonder if they'll eat my fins anyway…" this conversation on the dieting habits of the Slavercruds was then interrupted by several of the fat creatures walking up (or down since the Slavercruds were comming from the "top" of the Upside Down castle) the dungeon staircase towards them.

Milo who was still a bit shaky from his tornado ride considered opening the blue umbrella again but realized that the monstrous beasts so used to traveling in Zo's storms would simply catch them in the air. The drop off the top of the Castle dungeon was also a very long one with Rapsy too far away to catch them away before they were devoured by the Slavercruds or dashed against the rocky obsidian below.

"Hello!" Milo said doing the best thing he could think of. The man gave them a happy greeting with a tip of his umbrella waving in a salute.

"Grind you up and have your toes and faces for supper. Gnash you good. Beat you. Taste your bones in soup." The Slavercruds' dieting habits unfortunately, were not exaggerated by the Toadman jester. The Slavercruds didn't actually enjoy such things in their soup but to their mind when your unpopular already, you should be as unpopular as you possibly can be, and cannibalism certainly will do that.

"I don't think your reaching them." E. Bused said as they backed away from the salivating monsters that approached.

"I rather noticed. Here, Rapsy try this umbrella as I try one of the others…" Milo handed the Hissing Wing the yellow Winkie umbrella which the Hissing Wing

The Wooing of Ozma

raised high above his head. Milo considered trying the rainbow colored one out but wasn't sure that it was wise to waste it so soon.

When the folds of the Winkie Umbrella popped a beautiful stream of yellow light made a rainbow around Rapsy and gentle music, but otherwise the Hissing Wing's magical umbrella did nothing.

"Pppppfftt." E. Bused gave a gesture with his tongue. "That's a fairly useless power."

Milo then popped the Purple Umbrella and the Umbrella flew out of his hand into the sky where it promptly exploded like a rocket sending sparks all across Zo in what would have been a very powerful weapon had not Milo used it on the sky.

"Nice move Sherlock." E. Bused grabbed the Emerald Umbrella and popped it as a stream of emeralds poured out of the umbrella in great amounts on the ground where they sparkled and shined.

"Five umbrella's down…" Milo cursed "Oh the good man's life is full of light and the sinner's road dark and gloomy so we have done something…"

Milo stopped in his quotation when he heard the sound of the Slavercruds clapping at the show they were being given. Aside from having unhealthy diets and very smelly exteriors, Slavercruds love nothing more than shows of magic whether humbug or reality.

"Maybe I should sing a number to keep their attention on seeing us instead of eating us." Milo opened his mouth to sing a verse before E. Bused clasped his hand over Milo's mouth.

"Let's not." E. Bused then did a fantastic display of his dancing skill by performing a number out of the Wonderful Wizard of Oz by L. Frank Baum.

"Well white is the color of good and my favorite so we might as well try it now." Milo lifted up the next to last umbrella Glinda had enchanted for him.

Out popped from it a steady stream of magical poppy dust that hovered over the Slavercruds enjoying heartily E. Bused's dancing. The dust settled on the monster's eyes before each of the Slavercruds started to yawn and then slowly toppled over each other into a deep slumber. The White Umbrella had been enchanted with the pollen of the poppies around the Emerald City and it would be some time before the monsters woke up.

"Next time Massssssster you ssssshould try your favorite color firssssst." Rapsy suggested as E. Bused snored soundly at their feet along with the Slavercruds.

"Yes, perhaps. Well I suppose we should depart before these sad pathetic wretches wake up. Here help me carry E. Bused onto your back while I try and…" Milo with some difficulty mounted on top of Raspy and the group took once again to the air. Flying above the streets of Zo the rider and his mount spotted the very strange sight of many of Zo's citazens gathering in the town square. At the heart of the crowd was the most bizarre assortment of Oz citizens one was likely to see in any one place.

"Look! There is a crowd forming." Milo observed.

***

The Town Square of the Obsidian City was a very dark place like most of Zo but it was also one of the busiest with a huge statue of Princess Zo dominating the entire cluster. It was not a very pretty statue despite that Zoam for all of her cruelty was very pretty herself.

The Wooing of Ozma

The reason the statue was not very pretty was in part because it was so lifelike that everyone thought it might just as well be Princess Zoam about ready to turn the poor downtrodden people of Zo into something else at any moment. Given the popularity of this move yesterday today the vast majority of the people of Zo were gathered beneath the statue of Princess Zoam and hoping for some more of yesterday's miracles to occur. They were not to be disappointed.

"Hello." Princess Ozma said, opening the door that was at the base of Princess Zoam's statue's feet. Long ago the King of Zo, Zozo the Afraid to be precise, had decided that it would be good to escape the people if they ever rose up against him. He had thus had a huge tunnel dug from the bottom of his palace to the statue of his daughter in hopes of escaping them. Of course Zozo the Afraid would not long after be turned into a plant in the palace by Zoam but you'll be happy to know Zozo enjoyed being a plant much more than he enjoyed his original form. Certainly Zozo was glad that he wasn't beheaded and forced to sit with his dreary relatives. It was through his very tunnel that the Princess of Oz and her menagerie were coming up through to greet the people of Zo.

"Look! It is Princess Zoam!" the people said crowding around the Princess before the Snark Snark lifted her up in the air by his trunk and they were much startled. Princess Zoam could do many great things such as turn you into things, turn you into things, yell very loudly, stomp her feet so hard the ground shook, and turn you into things but flying was not one of the things she was known for.

Charles Phipps

"No! It is not!" Phil cried at the top of his lungs and everyone looked at the Black Spectacled Guardsman including his toothless long clawed wife and very greedy ugly children whom Philip gulped at seeing. "It is Princess Ozma of the Kingdom of Oz! Rightful ruler of the land who has come to conquer us and subjugate our people under her tyrannical rule!"

Ozma looked down at Phil. "I beg your pardon?"

"Sorry…it's the magic earmuffs. I'm used to hearing the opposite of what I mean so I say the opposite instead out of habit. I mean just and loving rule!" Phil the Revolutionary Council leader said. The effect on the crowd of Zo was immediate as everyone soon began to scratch their heads and wonder what exactly the famous soldier had said.

"What's just and loving mean?" Elmo the Mess Maker said, summing up the feelings of the Zo people.

Ozma looked at the Zo people in alarm because she had not expected that even in a land such as Zo there to be such a lack of basic understanding what it means to have a better life. Ozma searched her mind to try and figure out what sort of words would describe life under her rule instead of that of her evil cousins.

"It's just like ruler under Zoam save she'll turn us into anything we want," Gregor said proudly.

"Ummmm." Ozma looked down at the Guardsman. "I think it'll be more than that Gregor."

"HIP! HIP! HOOREY! ALL HAIL OZMA!" the reaction from the People of Zo was immediate and they soon were hailing their new queen with great fanfare, which in Zo, was mostly just groans and loud grunts. Ozma found it quite appalling that the people were so willing to give up their current queen for

The Wooing of Ozma

someone just off the streets with a few promises but given the alternative she supposed she couldn't blame their silliness.

A shadow soon passed over the girl queen ruler and she looked up to see a trio of descending figures into the edge of the crowd. Milo Starling who was looking quite dashing in his new Sunday (for that's what day it was) clothes despite they're now being soaked just as badly as his old ones had been. The Toad E. Bused, whom Ozma had yet to have the presence of mind to meet, was looking quite content despite a few bumps on the head. Finally the Hissing Wing Rapsy, of who Ozma was inclined to be testy with because of what he had nearly done to Dorothy, was looking joyous at surviving until their quest's end which meant many more crashes in the future.

"Oh hello Milo. What are you doing here?" Ozma asked as Phil tried to threaten Rapsy with his blunt ended spear.

Milo seeing the beautiful Princess Ozma gave her another sweeping bow and stood for several long moments staring at her beauty. Ozma seeing that the young man had gone into another one of his trances, wondered if she would have to wave her hand in front of his eyes to snap him out of it again before he came out of it on his own, saying "Ummm we've come to rescue you."

E. Bused and Rapsy frowned thinking that their efforts in rescuing the Princess had come a bit too late.

"Oh how very sweet," Ozma said to Milo and gave him a kiss upon the side of the cheek.

Milo turned a rather pleasant shade of red at that moment. He wasn't enchanted, angry, or embarrassed but simply very grateful for a token of affection from the Princess. "Well it's rather like this. Last night while I was singing outside your room…trying to sing…" Milo admitted "I was arrested by your very pleasant mechanical man for violating some form of wooing law and by the time I was brought forth for trial, you had already been replaced by Zoam, and…"

E. Bused put two webbed fingers in his mouth and gave a whistle. "Excuse me. I hate to interrupt you two but given that this is Zo the arguably most oppressive country in Fairydom I think we should probably work on getting you out of here. So let me give you the E. Bused shortened version of this. Zoam's captured and Milo wants to court you because he's convinced he is and probably is completely in love with you. If it's alright would you not have him locked up every time he tries to express that."

Milo looked at the Toadman jester who was already spinning on the top of his head upside down for no apparent reason. "Thank you E. Bused."

Ozma just looked at Milo as she put her hands together and tried to think about what she wanted to say. She remembered Prince Pompo and his proposal only seconds after they had met and frankly she wasn't anxious to repeat such a humiliating experience.

"Princess Ozma if it's all right with you may I have your permission to court you. I promise to Heaven I shall not sing again." Milo bowed. Ozma smiled at Milo and said.

"I'd very much like you to court me Milo and I'd very much like to court back." It was something, which was necessary in Oz court romance. Among mortals usually one person would court another with

The Wooing of Ozma

them expected to do it all but in Oz, both had to court each other or it was really an exercise in futility. It had led to a very large absence of traditional romance in Oz but surprisingly happy relationships when they did develop.

"That's wonderful," Milo declared even as squawking was heard in the background.

"Yes I think it is. Unfortunately we cannot leave until the Land of Zo has been brought under the Flag of Oz." Princess Ozma said looking into Milo's eyes.

Milo blinked for a moment and nodded with a light shake of his head "Well I suppose that's a very nice thing for you to do. May I offer my army's assistance?"

"Really, Milo you are really going to have to start asking us first. Sure Princess!" E. Bused shouted as the area around Princess Ozma, Milo, the Snark Snark, Rapsy, and the inhabitants of Zo were filled with hissing wings.

"Oh dear," Princess Ozma said before Milo put his hand on hers with a smile.

"I have a solution already for this Your Highness." Milo then handed Rapsy the Rainbow Umbrella and said. "I give you your freedom Rapsy and the one weapon of which can defeat the evil Rain Maker Igor. Use it well my noble knight to liberate your people and lead them well. For without wise leadership a nation is in trouble…" he smirked and finished "but with good counsellors there is safety."

Rapsy then lifted up his umbrella as the Hissing Wings shouted as one. "CAPTAIN RAPSY HAS AN UMBRELLA! HE IS THE NEW KING!" Unfolding the magical umbrella of Rainbows a most wonderful

Charles Phipps
thing happened that would change the lives of everyone in Zo forever.

The Wooing of Ozma

Chapter Thirteen

Rapsy the Hissing Wing was now quite sure that he was at the happiest time of his life. While he wasn't quite sure that the Hissing-Wings were a noble race yet, but he was quite sure that he was proving himself very noble by holding an umbrella and being lauded as the new King of Zo. "I wish all of you could live in a land as wonderful and joyous as the one I just visited!"

Rapsy said as he popped the rainbow umbrella. These proved to be a most magical choice of words because the umbrella began to spin wildly before launching itself into the air at their recitation.

The Lady Glinda had put her most powerful enchantment on the Rainbow Umbrella and that was a single wish granted to someone with pure intention.

Wishes are dicey things and you never know whether or not your going to get you want when you make them. Whoever looks after wishes in the Cosmos was feeling sympathetic that day however, because the result of the wish was nothing sort of spectacular.

"Oh my." The Snark Snark blinked and the big furry elephant with wings and bullhorns was briefly visible under the showers of Yellow, White, Red,

Purple, Green, and Blue light that followed the umbrella as it encircled all of Zo. The Umbrella soon reached the top of Zo and exploded like a rocket on the Fourth of July. Wherever the magical dust of its' remains hit the people and objects of the dark breakaway of Oz were transformed.

The ugly obsidian which made most of the city was transformed into clear beautiful crystal, the beaten down people's of Zo's drab clothing were suddenly turned into startlingly vibrant shades of every color of the rainbow. The Slavercruds so fast asleep ontop of the Castle Dungeon were transformed into their distant cousins the Sweetnergs, which neither smelled nor turned people into soup. All around the City of Zo what was horrible, mean, and vile was made into something that you could be proud of. Even the Volcano was transformed into a lovely snow capped mountaintop and the storm over Oz at last dissipated with the weather machine in Igor's Tower exploding with a boom.

Milo having never seen anything quite so startling as this before looked upon the changes to Zo in a mixture of awe and fear.

E. Bused looked at it with a bit more of a cynical of an eye. "Well, now that Zo is conquered can we get going?"

Ozma pointed at the sole remaining part of Zo that was as ugly as it was before. The Tower of Igor was protected by magic and thus only partially affected by Glinda's greater magic. Though it no longer was pumping its evil chemicals and white smoke poured out of its smokestack instead of black, it was still an intact visible symbol of Zo's former evil. "We can go once we've taken that tower and arrested Igor for his crimes."

It took a great deal to rankle the Princess of Oz but being stuffed in cold iron cage so someone could take over her kingdom was among the things that upset her.

"Well you certainly don't ask for much your Highness. Pick a card, any card." E. Bused conjured a deck of 51 cards.

The Wooing of Ozma

"The Queen of Hearts," Ozma said looking at it.

"No you're not supposed…" E. Bused sighed and put away his 50 remaining Queen of Hearts cards.

Ozma lifted up then Milo's emerald umbrella and placed it above the Hissing Wing Rapsy's head before saying. "Do you swear to uphold Oz's laws, be a just and noble king, and treat all your people's problems as your own?"

Rapsy bowed before Princess Ozma and said "Yesssssssss Your Majesty."

"Then I crown you Rapsy the First, King of Zo under Oz." Ozma gave a glittering smile that was so beautiful, E. Bused wished he had sunglasses.

Audible clapping filled with the town square of Zo and the Statue of Zoam transformed with a glow of white energy into a petite statue of Princess Ozma. Phil, the new leader of the Successful Revolution Post-Transformation Council, handed the Queen a gold and emerald Oz flag from where the white and black of Zo once flew and the Princess raised it above her head as she was lifted once again on the back of her Snark Snark mount. Together the group formed a very large army for the taking of the Tower of the Last Weather Master of Zo.

"That was very nice of you to give the Hissing Wing ruler ship over Zo Princess Ozma," the Snark Snark said bouncing along merrily with the marching legion of dogooders.

"Rulership is a great burden dear Snark Snark. I have done Rapsy the First, Hissing Wing King of Zo no favors by putting him as ruler of a people who will have to learn how to love, share, and care for one another as in all civilized kingdoms. However Oz is whole again and with our aid I am sure eventually the heart of Zo will become as beautiful as its appearence."

Princess Ozma smiled as potted roses were lifted off a nearby windowsill as a gift to her by one of the Zo children.

"I see. Can I be a king sometime?" The Snark Snark questioned not really understanding at all.

"I'll discuss it with Burgomeister Bumhug." Ozma replied. The shadow of the evil tower of Igor Lackey came ever closer with repressive menace.

***

Igor Lackey crawled out of the wreckage of the Machine he had spent decades building. While for an immortal being that wasn't so much time, Igor didn't like to repeat things. The Weather Master of Zo wasn't exactly sure what had happened but he had been preparing to drench the entire town of Bunbury in a soggy flood when the dials and gauges had overloaded in a huge detonation. Igor's laboratory was a mess with all of his bottles, books of magic, powders, and machines scattered about the remnants of the Weather-making machine. Smoke was fluttering around and the smell of oil and rain water heavy in the air.

"Mother!" Igor shouted at the top of his lungs before he heard the most curious sound coming from the outside. "Singing?" Igor said aloud and opened the windows to see what exactly was occurring.

Igor stared in openmouthed astonishment at the changes that had happened to his beloved Zo. Where once had been a austere, depressing, and otherwise

The Wooing of Ozma

proper kingdom there was now a shining monument to Oz. Life in the Lackey family had always been difficult. Your family just as often as not included monsters like Gorgons, Growleywogs, and Harpies as often as people.

Birthdays or Christmas were not occasions for parties but instead funerals or some other person's misfortune. You had to learn your basic spells by the age of five or you'd be fed to the family beasts and if you couldn't curse someone by the age of thirteen, you were turned into a polecat. It made the Lackeys a very small but very animal friendly family. It had been for this reason that Zo was the perfect home for them after they'd been driven out of Oz. Now that it had changed Igor knew his family's time in Zo was coming to an end.

"Mother!" Igor shouted again as his mother did not appear. The Weather Master of Zo spotted Ozma riding on the back of an invisible creature, probably a Snark Snark, comming towards his tower. Grabbing his magical briefcase Igor began loading all of his books, wands, cups, charts, machine spare parts, pictures of Zoam, unbroken chemistry tubes, cages for his raven familiars, and the Book of Records inside it. Unfortunately despite pushing on it, jumping on it, and beating it with a club, Igor was unable to force Glinda's magical volume in the full briefcase and simply tossed it aside in the end. Snapping his luggage shut Igor grabbed his enchanted broom and prepared to fly out the window down to Oz rather than face the daughter of Lurline. Before Igor did he spotted his mother and stared in open mouthed astonishment for the second time today.

Charles Phipps

His Mother had undergone a transformation of her own thanks to Raspy's wish.

"Mother!" Igor screeched and looked at the beautiful long blonde haired woman in her twenties. Agatha the Lovely was dressed in a shimmering white gown and looked completely human but for a pretty pair of butterfly wings on her back. The smile on her face would have melted any heart but the twisted and black one of Igor Lackey, which I might add was already given to Princess Zoam. You could find it in a metal box on her mantle piece in her bedroom next to her Father's portrait but that is neither here nor there.

"Hello Igor! I was just standing outside on the tower rooftop when a most wondrous change overcame me! Aren't I beautiful?" Agatha Lackey asked looking into a nearby mirror as she fluffed her hair slightly.

"Whatever. Mother in a few minutes a large group of very unhappy people are going to be storming our Castle just like they did to Uncle Victor a few years ago. If you'd be so kind enough to hold them off during this particular encounter, I'll go flying out the window and leave you to your fate," Igor said to his mother. The ex-Weather Maker thought this was a most fair deal.

"Sure. Go right ahead," Agatha replied as she gazed longingly at her reflection.

Igor, before he left, went to fetch the one thing he had never wanted to use but was perhaps his best option for revenge. Grabbing the iron bottle containing his father's Universal Anti-Magical Solvent Igor held it close to his chest and leapt onto his broom, sailing out of the window.

The Wooing of Ozma

Agatha did not notice the escape of Igor but when she turned away from her reflection the former Harpy did notice that a number of Igor's magical vials were covered in dust.

"Oh dear. Some of Igor's Powder of Mix-Up seems to have fallen on their labels. Oh well I'm sure it's nothing too important to keep me from my beloved reflection for any length of time."

***

With Igor having so cowardly fled the scene of his crimes, there was very little for Princess Ozma to do upon arrival. Ozma decided that the first order of business was to gather up what tools of magic that Igor had left behind and have them either destroyed or bundled up for transport down to Oz. The Weather Machine of Zo she instructed would be rebuilt as best the people of Zo knew how to do but only used to give people rain where they needed it and fix the sky when it was in danger of causing disaster.

"What are we going to do about her Your Royal Highness?" Phil the former Revolutionary Council head, former post Revolutionary Council head, now present Prime Minister in Charge of Ozzification asked as he pointed to the ex-Harpy Agatha who was still gazing at her reflection.

"I do not believe she will cause much more trouble for the people of Zo so long as she has her mirror. Just in case she ever gets tired of her reflection though I think you should make her a member of the court Rapsy. There she can force everyone to dress in elaborate costumes and themed parties whenever real business should be done. It will vent her evil

Charles Phipps

impulses," Ozma said, looking at the mother of the warlock.

"You assssssssk much of ussssssss Queen Ozzzzzzma." Rapsy said as he, Gregor, and Phil winced at the prospects of court life.

"I'm not a Queen," Ozma said quite resolutly before she stopped to think about the words for a moment and smiled lightly "Yet."

E. Bused looked at Milo as the two of them prepared Princess Ozma's magic circle which would allow her to teleport everyone from Oz back down to their homes in a single instant. It would be very hard without the wishing belt but Ozma had insisted that she could do it with what was in the Laboratory.

Milo was currently rambling on passages in the Good Book which dealt with the supernatural because E. Bused had unfortunately to his considerable displeasure asked about it an hour previous. Milo you see felt the need to defend his new found love against the rather odd charges occasionally levied by his fellows against the Land of Oz and that delightful Mr. Potter Milo was so fond of.

"…and that passage specifically dealt with poison dealers but even that was invalidated by the much more preferable new writings. Not anywhere in the book however does it say that a man should not nor could possibly defy his true heart for a fairy maiden Which just goes to show it is common sense all al…" Milo was then interrupted by E. Bused whistling in his ear.

"Ahhhhh you have something to say E. Bused?" Milo felt his ear in pain.

The Wooing of Ozma

"Yes I've finally decided what I want to be turned into." E. Bused smiled and looked proudly at his perhaps only real friend until today. Of course Milo had only been his friend as of yesterday but he was off to a good start he thought for only two days. How many friends have you saved from certain peril after all?

"Very well, you should tell her what you wished to be turned into." Milo made a 'shoo shoo' gesture while the Toad Man bounced up to the Princess.

"Princess Ozma I've decided what I'd like you to turn me into," E. Bused said as he pulled out a burning torch, a sword, and a living chicken and began to juggle them over one leg.

Princess Ozma blinked wondering when she had promised to turn anybody into anything. However despite her distaste for transformations she found that there had been too far much trouble in Zo and if it would make him happy she'd turn him into anything short of a hydra or cat eating blood guzzler.

"I'd like to be turned into...absolutely nothing," The Toadman Jester announced as Ozma took the chicken away from him and set the dizzy bird down on the ground where she could walk away free.

Ozma looked at the toadman with an odd look. "You don't want to be turned into anything?"

The Toadman shook his head proudly. "With this new form I'm already better off than the evil finger eating Munchkin people. Plus I am distinctly unique enough as it is but have someone similar enough in the Frogman to play crazy person to his straight man. Which is a much more interesting use of my jesting abilities than being turned into things I think." The

Charles Phipps

Frogman of course E. Bused had found could only tell the truth and the jester had hopes of convincing him to team together for a swamp playing comedy troupe.

Ozma smiled "I'll have to introduce you to Ojo. Very well, Court Jester it is. By perchance do you know any puns?" They were Ozma's favorite type of joke though strangely the other members of her court usually got physically ill whenever she brought them up.

"Oh puns? Can't stand em. I do however have a vast repository of jokes! Why did the Chicken cross the road for instance! I dunno! Zoam turned him into a ashtray before I could ask him!" E. Bused smirked.

"Perhaps we should change your first name to something which starts with A and replace the last two letters of your name with an ive," Ozma said as she had a funny feeling that court was going to get much less funny thanks to the Toadman. It was not time to think on such matters though and Ozma proceeded to gather herself for the spell that would bring them all out of Zo.

Ozma performed the spell admirably.

The Wooing of Ozma
Chapter Fourteen

The celebration of Oz's defeat of its invaders (again) was another heralded event in the many heralded land of Ozma. Ozma Week, which had been mostly rained out, was now being heralded as becoming a annual national holiday due to Princess Ozma's defeat of the terrible invading Zo storm. The Ozites were even so kind as to remember those people who helped her do it like Whatshisname and Youknow who had important parts in it with Milo, the Snark Snark, and Raspy. The Land of Oz had not too hurt by the rainstorm but many new lakes had appeared along with rivers and ponds.

It would be a tireless effort from Oz's elite carpentry core, assembled by the Tin Woodsman, to fix all the damage that had been done. The Tin Woodsman himself promised to aid in the efforts for as long as possible which was not as troubling to him as you might suspect because the Woodsman had to live with the Scarecrow in his Corncob house until his Castle could be shined, oiled, and otherwise removed of all the rust that had appeared on it. The Tin Woodsman loved the Scarecrow as a brother and Scraps was the closest woman in Oz to his heart but it's hard to manage a kingdom from inside a vegetable.

For those among you who love animals I'm happy also to report that with the care of Aunt Em and the Medicine Man's care the sick multi-legged population from tiny Toto to large Hank expected to make a swift recovery.

Charles Phipps

The only real casualties of Zo's storm would have to be the Paint people of the previously unknown Oz kingdom of Watercolorloo. Mixed together by the unexpected rainstorm the entire region has since gone to resemble a hopeless mish mash of colors. Depressed, the remaining paint people have taken to drinking coffee in bookstores and debating sullen meaning in their bizarre landscape of ruined paintings. Hopefully in a few years some new colors would be born in the region and it can move away from it's black period.

"All's well that ends well Princess. Are you absolutely sure that you want to court this young man back who is courting you?" Glinda asked the Princess of Oz in the Royal Ballroom. Both were taking a break from the rather large amount of dancing going on. The Magic Phonograph had finally gotten some halfway decent records and was playing a lively five step in the emerald draped Hall blessed with countless rainbow colored windows to the outside world. Ozma had spent the entire afternoon dancing but had reserved most of her dances for Milo. Once the young man had taken some of the Wogglebug's waltz, the Wogglebug (like the Jitterbug only more scholarly), dosey-do, and tap dance pills he was quite light on his feet.

"Yes I do. I think we get along very well together. If not destined eternal love then a even closer friendship than we already now share will emerge from it. Hopefully soon with kissing. Grrr, darn laces!" Ozma frowned and blushed at her cussing (darn being an awful word you know) as she tried to get the green emerald dancing slippers on right.

The Wooing of Ozma

"Well there are formalities to observe regarding mortal and fairy relations Princess. However, if you feel this way then I am happy for you both and wish you many happy millennium. No. Princess, you have to go over, under, then…no your doing it all wrong," Glinda sighed gesturing with her wand to direct the Princess. Finally, Ozma tapped the shoes with her wand and they tied themselves.

"I know it's cheating but I want to get back to dancing," Ozma explained as she got up off the bench. It was then that the ballroom filled with bright vivid colors of red, yellow, blue, and green as a very august personage arrived at the front doors of the celebration.

"Daddy!" Polychrome shouted and ran to the figure, which had appeared so suddenly.

King Prism the Too-Many-Numbers-To-Count (because he adds one every time a rainbow appears anywhere in the World) was a beautiful figure if a very strange one. Standing roughly four feet seven inches, the Rainbow in his human form had a short red beard and a jolly twinkle in his eye. The man was completely bald on the top of his head but with the redness of his skin it did not make him less handsome but gave more character to his looks. King Prism was dressed in a fabulous suit of white with a cape of every conceivable color draping heavily behind him.

"Polychrome my dear!" King Prism hugged his daughter, who thankfully had inherited her features mainly from her mother despite the beauty of the Rainbow Fairy King.

Ozma walked over to the Rainbow and smiled as she saw outside the windows of the Emerald Palace a huge bow of colors was arched over Oz like there never had been before. Oz had seen rainbows before but the one that King Prism shined now onto Oz was brighter and more lovely than any that had ever appeared before.

"When I send clouds over the earth, the rainbow will be seen in the clouds and I will remember my promise to you and to every other being that never again shall floods come and destroy all life." Milo gazed upon the monument and recited a very particular passage that was dear to him and which Polychrome and King Prism were fond of as well.

"Who died though?" E. Bused asked though, and ruined the moment. Thankfully it wasn't completely ruined because of course no one did die in the invasion which was the happiest part of it all.

"Indeed I have agreed to shine a wondrous rainbow over the Land of Oz this evening for my daughter's friends. I have not shined like this over a land for many many years. The joy that fills me for seeing those abusers of rain and light get what's coming to them is enough to make me shine ten times my usual self." Prism smiled dancing and soon Polychrome's sisters Dew, Sunbeam, and Reflection were sailing down the rainbow to join in the dance as well. Needless to say the young men of Oz who got a chance to dance with the beautiful sky faeries felt very lucky indeed. None could keep up with their partners who had danced across the sky since light and water first met. "Where exactly are the Wicked Princess of Zo and her chief crony anyway?" King Prism asked as he started dancing a Russian gig around Ozma while he talked.

Ozma spun around in circles so much that she felt alittle dizzy talking to the Sky Fairy. "My cousin I

The Wooing of Ozma

have stripped of her kingdom so she is no longer a Princess of Zo let alone Oz and she currently sits powerless over yonder." Ozma gestured to a corner where Princess Zoam despite her great beauty sat alone. The fact she'd tried to turn the last three men who asked her to dance into pigeons had soured her reputation a bit.

"It is my decision that as family she will be able to remain in Oz for the rest of eternity if she desires..." Ozma let out a heavy sigh. Ozma was not looking forward to sharing the same home with such an unpleasant personage for the thousand or so years it would probably take to teach her good manners. "She'll be fed the Wizard's special tonic every day to keep her from using her powers for evil as well. As for Igor Lackey, I'm afraid he escaped and is bound to cause trouble in the future."

King Prism smiled and nodded "Tis more than such a nasty Unseelie Royal deserves, it is. As for Lackey, his family always has caused trouble and always will I fear."

No sooner had Ozma heard those words, that a great commotion came from the very doors that they were in front of which burst open to a most unexpected sight. Hovering a full five feet off the ground on top of a broomstick was Igor Lackey clutching the green whiskers of Omby Amby. The Royal Army of Oz was following along in obvious pain from being dragged by those very same whiskers. In Igor's other hand was a cold iron bottle and Glinda upon seeing it, immediately shoved Ozma behind her in a protective stance.

"We have a visitor Your Highness!" Omby Amby tried to recover his dignity as best he could.

Charles Phipps

"Let go of him this instant!" Ozma shouted to the Weather Master as she walked from behind Glinda.

"Igor! You've come to enslave my captors!" Zoam said happily as she jumped to her feet. She thought this sounded much more dramatic than 'You've come to rescue me!' you see.

"Yes Your Currently In a Bit Of A Spotness!" Igor threw the Soldier with Green Whiskers on the ground by his whiskers then uncorked the bottle. "I have come to take the Princess Zoam from your hands and I will utterly destroy Oz if you do not immediately comply!"

"I think you will not!" Milo who was feeling awfully heroic came up behind Ozma along with a large number of very powerful and very strange people who might have destroyed Igor then and there if not for the natural inclinnation of people in Oz toward being polite. It's why Oz is such a nice place since most other places arn't to rude warlocks threatening them with death.

"I would hear what he has to say Princess Ozma for that bottle I recognize as the creation of a most wicked and vile Alchemist." Glinda said. "Inside it is the essence of mundanity and the potion is powerful enough that if it is emptied here in the center of Oz, it will reach across Oz and eradicate everything magical here. We will all be reduced to powerless mortals condemned to die."

"But if you do that Igor you'll become powerless and die too! Not to mention your beloved Zoam!" Ozma stared at the man who was frankly showing himself to be more stupid than she ever gave him credit for. Princess Ozma had been giving him a great deal of credit for being stupid as well.

The Wooing of Ozma

"Beloved Zoam? Sheesh and I thought I had poor taste in girls!" E. Bused said having very recently made the aquaintence of an attractive girl of the Much Feared Munchkins.

Zoam soon had rushed to the side of Igor's magical broomstick as she bounded past Tik-Tok, the Tin Woodsman, The Tin Soldier, the Snark Snark, and the Woozy who it turns out had some common ancestry. "It doesn't matter as long as we're able to destroy so much happiness." Zoam looked into her lover's deliciously evil eyes as if for the first time and they knew they'd be in love as long as they spent their time hurting other people. In other words the pair would be in love forever. "Destroy them milord and we'll conquer them once their powerless," Zoam suggested as she displayed her enormous grasp of logic.

Igor, as always, had a greater grasp. "I won't pour the potion Glinda if your Princess Ozma allows myself and Princess Zo to leave with our magic intact. We shall go to whatever realm we desire to cause whatever mischief we may, for as long as we both may live." Igor wasn't very keen on Zoam continuing to cause trouble if he dissapeared, so he accented the both part.

Ozma stared at the bottle which reaked such chilling evil that she actually shivered in its' presence. Evile Lackey had formed it from the loss of innocence, the remnants of imaginary friends, a heart turned to stone, the hair of a zealot among many other noxious ingredients. The sound of wailing and cries of anger, pain, and for swift thoughtless action seemed to go forth from the bottle and she had no doubt in her mind a single drop of that substance could destroy the Emerald City. It was a difficult decision but Ozma

Charles Phipps

knew that others would face these troublemakers if they were deprived of this weapon.

"On the condition that you turn over the potion to us and promise to never use or develop such a weapon again." Ozma said very coolly as her friends gathered round her. It was very painful to give in to evil but she couldn't allow all the people in Oz to die of old age, nor could she let purely magical beings as the Scarecrow and Tik-Tok be destroyed. Warm caring hands touched Ozma and she looked up at her friends who embraced her, they understood even if she did not entirely.

It occurred to Igor to agree, grab Zoam, then toss the potion on the ground to destroy Oz but it was possible that his love for Zoam had managed to awaken what little good there was sleeping inside of him. "Agreed." Igor said as he turned the potion over to Glinda who promptly stoppered up the evil potion.

"You should have just zapped them all," Zoam murmured even as Igor got off his broom (which was only sized for one) and led his fairy bride down the halls of the Emerald Palace until they were in the heart of the Courtyard.

"Patience Your Wickedness. I have no intention of honoring any deals to Oz. By Yurline the Queen of all Evil Fey.I intend to leave only so long as it takes to raise a new army to capture Zo and this place." Igor made a terrible oath by the eviliest of all beings. Sadly what good was awakened in him didn't stay awake very long.

"What shall we do first then my love?" Princess Zoam said with a smile,

The Wooing of Ozma

absolutely infuriated beyond belief that anyone would dare take her prisoner and loving the idea of revenge for it. That her kingdom had been taken hardly bothered her as it just gave her more people to hurt because of it.

"We shall journey back to Zo and undo all the changes that Princess Ozma has wrought. She has turned your kingdom upside down your Soon to be as Fearsome as Beforeness. Once we've kicked Raspy off your throne..." Igor started to say as he fiddled with his briefcase of magic and withdrew a bag of what he thought was teleporting powder.

"Raspy? That disgusting beast thinks he can rule my kingdom?" Princess Zoam said in infuriated anger. "I'll feed him to the Harpies!"

"We'll need to find more of those Your Majesty. Once we've retaken Zo, we'll take it all over the world to the Dark Places like Boogeyland and the Kingdom of the Restless Dead. We'll gather up an army of the most fearsome evils that have never been seen the like of in Oz. We'll build weapons like the ones mortals have that kill indiscriminately and burn forests like paper and soon not a trace will remain of those who dared harm you!" Igor was truly not that interested in doing such monstrous things but the talk of them obviously made Zo happy.

"To Zo!" Zoam smiled and clapped her hands together.

"To Zo!" Igor said clutching his bride in a hug as he tossed the magical powder over them both. For a second a huge green flash filled the palace gardens and afterwards where both of the tyrants had stood, there now stood a single intertwined tree. Igor had mistakenly used his Powder of Oak Transformation on them both and thus the threat to Oz was ended. An uglier tree there never was in the Palace Gardens but few residents of Oz were unhappy to see it there instead of the now defeated Weather Makers of Zo running free.

Because Zoam is family, Princess Ozma makes sure it's well watered and fertilized.

***

After that night's ball (and the events which went with it) both Milo and Ozma retired to the Royal Library where they began to read over the laws regarding relationships between faeries and mortals. As a rule, faeries absolutely love mortals to death and few get through eternity without having one catch their eye. Unfortunately, given that faeries and humans are literally from two different worlds (much like men and women) those in fairy country have come up with just as many rules for relationships as there are in our for men and women in our own world. They also work about as well, which is to say not at all.

"A man who wishes to court a leprechaun lass must agree to forego all claims on her father's pot of gold and place a bowl of milk out for the Family Fox every Thursday," Milo read aloud from a very large book with a shamrock emblazoned upon it.

Ozma looked up from her own tome, which had been personally written up for Lurline's court many years earlier. Ozma had remembered being the daughter of Lurline the Fairy Queen when her enchantment as the boy Tip was broken. Her true father had long ago been King of Oz before it was

The Wooing of Ozma

enchanted and she herself was half mortal. Lurline had asked Ozma to rule Oz when his own many great grand nephew King Pastoria had been without a child to take over when he died. Because the Princess was shrunk down to a child's size and raised by Pastoria, she was her own great grandaunt which was amusing if not terribly helpful in figuring out how to love a mortal man.

"I don't think your going to find anything in there about our having a relationship Milo. Oooo I found it!" Ozma said pointing to a particular passage one that referred to full and half-blooded fairy royalty loving mortals involved or going to be involved in religious professions. "It's extremely relevant as well."

"What does it say?" Milo said looking over her shoulder into the tome.

"It says that in order to prove a worthy true heart for a fey a mortal of this profession must hold fast to his innocence, love of life, sing her praises every day, and love her with all of his heart for a period of not less but more at wooee's request of nine hundred years before true lovers' hearts be joined forever...." Ozma said the number then blinked. "Oh my that's a lot of years. I suppose it's to compensate for the longevity of my race."

Milo's eyes widened at the mentioning of the number of years that was being ascribed to the courting process.

"Is it too long?" Ozma trusted her ancestors' judgment but hated to disappoint a friend who seemed so obviously enamored of her. Still if he was not willing to go the nine hundred years she was certain he could remain her friend. True love she was certain would conquer all even a man who would have to do this. Ozma noticed that Milo's gaze was softening into a beatific smile as he looked upon her and got on one knee.

"Milady, the ancient Methuselah lived nine hundred years and his ancestor longer still. If I may live for you that long then I most certainly shall." Milo rose up and took her by the hands, they were surprisingly warm in his and she realized she was blushing. "Too often I have seen couples in my land rush into the most grand union of souls before they are ready and suffer greatly for it. They miss out on the knowing one another as friend and every inch of their spirits. I welcome this opportunity to do what no couple has, that I know of, before to prove my devotion"

Ozma smiled at her consort and said "So if I find a way out of this law you wouldn't take it up?"

"I did not say that my Princess," the words came naturally and Ozma knew it was correct. Milo and his umbrella would wait as long as possible for her heart and take what joy he could in her love as surely as a wife. Marriage was planning very far in the future but then again so was nine hundred years. The essence of growing up was accepting one's responsibility for things.

While Ozma had done so with her kingdom she now had to accept her responsibility to another. She was partially owned by the love they shared and he was owned partially by it. Gazing longingly into each other's eyes they shared their first kiss... and Ozma smiled as the clock struck the midnight of her body's sixteenth birthday

ABOUT THE AUTHOR

Charles Phipps came to Oz relatively late in his life, at least compared to those who grew up reading about L. Frank Baum's wonderful creation. Introduced to the books by a causal acquaintance, he soon fell in love with all the wondrous things that every one of the forty-plus series contained. Finally deciding that he had to write a book of his own, he settled on his favorite character Ozma and what he felt was always a travesty about her. "Ozma was always the most compassionate and sweet character in the story and it saddened me that she didn't have someone to love," Charles told at least one friend. That one idea eventually skyrocketed into a full trilogy and plans for more.

Charles Phipps is a student at Ohio University's Southern Campus in Ironton, Ohio and working toward a position as a history professor. His interests include folklore and mythology, comparative religion, and medieval history.

Printed in the United Kingdom
by Lightning Source UK Ltd.
9575700001B